Basic Threat

MARINA MOTAMED

Title: Basic Threat
Author: Marina Motamed
Illustrator: Ankit R.

ISBN 978-1-915557-06-3
eISBN 978-1-915557-07-0

Firouz Media Limited
www.firouzmedia.com
IG: @firouzmedia

BASIC THREAT

CHAPTER ONE

It's the beginning of another day for April, a day she's not so happy about. A day so dreaded, it makes her limbs go numb. It is a Thursday, a school day, and she is not in the mood. Yet, she slides out of bed, lazily, and trudges to the window, looking out of it. The day is still coming alive, as the sun covers the rooftop of houses with orange rays of light, like a fine orange sheet. Everyone is awake, birds are fluttering from one tree to another, searching for what they would eat, or where they would perch. April yawns, and opens up the window frames, the humid smell of pine trees and grasses hit her in the face, she takes it in, and sighs. 'What another day,' she said to herself.

She couldn't help but look down on the little heads of a passing crowd as their voices rise up to the sky, filling the morning atmosphere with chants and words of clamor, as they match, like ants in a single file, with raised placards of different colors in their hands. As they walked through the streets, they could be heard screaming words such as, "Down with the nerds!" "The nerds need to go, they have no place in our town!" "Go back to your fancy shithole you call home, Einsteins!"

And on the placards, inscriptions like, "WE DO NOT WANT YOU ANYMORE!" "THEY CALL THEM-

SELVES NERDS, MORE LIKE NUMPS," "WE ARE FINE WITHOUT YOU!"

These are the words that were written on those pink, white, green placards, carried by the people below, protesting and matching to a rally where they would all speak against the nerds, smart individuals who help shape the society they live in.

"Great, another protest. When will they give up? It is not their fault they are what they are," April says under her breath, leaving the window side. She enters the bathroom as she has school to go to.

In a way, they won't give up. They do not seem like giving up, and might never give up. To them, this is like fighting for their rights, right to do as they please, to live as they like, without obstructions or regulations, without some smart guy telling them this is bad, or this should be done this way. They wanted total freedom of thought, and expression, but felt they weren't getting it, they felt the smart people who often entered their city were always in their way, they were like the police. And this has made them demand that they should be stopped from distorting their daily lives. They were tired of feeling like fools.

A voice comes through the door, "April, wake up! It's time for school!" The voice says to her. It's her mum.

"I am already up, mum… jeezzz," she screams from the bathroom.

Downstairs, she enters to meet her parents and brother already having breakfast. A plate of scrambled eggs and bacon is placed before her younger brother, with a glass cup of orange juice, her dad has the same thing on his plate, and her mum has a plate for herself also, though she's still in front of the cooker, making more bacon.

"Good morning, mum … Good morning, dad," she says to her parents, taking a seat at the dining table. They reply her, and she peers at her younger brother, as though expecting something from him, but he doesn't seem to notice as he continues to have his breakfast. "Good morning, Damien, since you want me to say it first," she said mockingly.

Damien raises his head to meet her, "Good morning, April, I am sorry I didn't see you there," he says, taking up a spoonful of scrambled eggs into his mouth.

She looks at him, getting herself ready to eat her breakfast, "It's alright."

The mum, Dareen, comes to meet them, and takes a seat beside her husband, April's father, Morris. She extends her hand and takes the jug of orange juice on the table, she pours it into her cup, and begins munching away on the eggs and bacon. For a moment, everyone seems to be focused on their food, until their mum decided to speak.

"Well, hope you all are enjoying the breakfast I made this morning?" she asks them, running her eyes round the table, sipping a cup of juice.

"Yes, mum," Damien said with a smile, raising his index finger in a thumbs-up.

She is delighted hearing Damien's reply, and looks toward April and her husband, but they didn't as much raise their heads, not to mention replying her question. She shrugs it off anyway.

"Did anyone see the rally outside? I think this is the 4th this week, right?" she asks.

"Actually, it's the 5th one this week, and it seems like they aren't going to stop anytime soon," says Morris, looking toward the window.

He could see the protesters in the blurry images the cream-colored curtain made as they walked past. They were still matching down their street, their voices as audible as ever, although not as audible as when April had opened her window. And they were still saying the same thing April had heard in her room, "Down with the nerds … We don't need 'em."

"Well, that kind of serves those know-it-alls right. If they weren't all over our business, telling us how to and how not to do things, acting as though without them, we would be lost, it just isn't fair, you know," Dareen says complacently.

"You are right, honey, they do not deserve a place here. They are always the ones taking up good spots in corporate businesses. And I know such positions can be demanding, I still believe we should be given a chance to prove ourselves," Morris says, confirming Dareen's words.

"Exactly what I am saying. And I hope the mayor listens this time," says Dareen with a forlorn expression.

As they talked, April and Damien said nothing on the table. Not that they couldn't, but they weren't just interested in what their parents were saying. They also knew how the nerds weren't liked in their city, and were often told by a lot of people to stay off many a time whenever they came to help someone, yet, it doesn't matter to them, April and Damien, that all these were happening right before their eyes. April, in particular, can't seem to shake off this feeling that being with the nerds was actually a good thing, but amidst the tempest of raw querulous emotions, her mind still thinks the nerds are better done away with.

Done with her food, she picks up her bag, and makes to leave, "Well, if you don't like them so much, why don't you go join the protest, mum and dad," she says sarcastically, leaving the table.

"Oh no, that is not the way we want our lives to be, April honey," she says, rising a bit from her seat, and raising her voice over Damien's head. When she was done, she sat back down, "It is bad enough we have a lot of angry folks who openly express their hate toward these people, I wouldn't want us to be part of them, don't you agree, dear?" she adds, cutting into the remaining bacon on her plate.

"You got that right, Dareen. It is better we act as though we are okay with them, so we do not come off as haters."

"Exactly, and remember this, Damien, on no account should you show contempt toward the smart people. Act normal, and be yourself. You hear me, boy?"

"Yes, mum," he answers calmly, looking out the window too.

"Now, finish up your breakfast before you run late for school," Dareen tells him.

On April's way to school, a girl runs toward her, and when she comes close enough, she jumps on April, startling her a little.

She gasps, and takes a look at her right, a girl with round, chestnut eyes, an oval face, and a wide smile revealing her neat set of teeth, has her hands over her neck. Her brown hair is left free over her shoulders, as it rises with the wind as they walk. She is wearing a bright yellow sweatshirt and green, military-style pants on black sneakers. April sees her, and she starts laughing, "Reilly, you silly goose," she says.

"Good morning, April Morris, how are you doing this morning?" Reilly asks, putting her arm round April's neck as they walk.

"Almost dead," she replies.

Reilly's face grimacing in confusion, she asks, "Why is that?"

"Well, first, this protest, and second, you almost gave me a heart attack!" she replies.

"Oh, someone's scared, I see," Reilly laughs, her dentures gleaming in the sunlight, "But, what about the protest? Isn't it a good thing they are calling out the hypocrisy of the seaside folks?" she asks.

"Yes, but isn't it getting too much? I mean, what if it is a good thing to have them around? You know, help us when we need them, that sort of thing," says April, looking into the crowd.

"Whatever help they want to give, I am pretty sure we

can do it ourselves," Reilly says, blinking her eyes very fast. "Besides, what have they got that we don't?" asks Reilly, as she took her arm away from April.

"Uhh, the ability to learn stuff faster than us,"

"If that's the case, we will learn as well, no matter how long it takes us. Please, I, Reilly Summers, will like to see a day when the nerds stay on their own, in their own town."

"Whatever, Reilly."

April is in a class awaiting the arrival of their History teacher, who would be taking them to their morning class. As she sits and thinks of the kind of lessons the teacher will give, his questions, and her failure in answering them, a guy in her class approaches her. She hasn't been much interested in guys lately.

"What's up, April, whatcha doing?" he asks, standing over her.

April takes up her head to meet the towering figure that has just shown up at her desk, her eyes becoming a slit on her face, mostly due to the sunlight behind him, "Nothing. Just waiting for the one-and-a-half hour of torture that is the class we are about to have," she says, looking forward before turning her face upward again, in a smile.

"Yeah, crazy, huh?"

"It sure is, Nigel."

"Yeah, I was thinking, April, if we can —"

Just then, their morning class teacher walks in, and Nigel has to leave April's desk for his.

"I guess we will talk later then," Nigel says, putting his hands in his pockets to cover up his nervousness.

"I guess so, Nigel," she replies to him with a smile again.

"Good morning, students, our topic today will be on the life of Alexander the Great, and how he became one of the greatest men history has ever known," says a plump man with protruding belly, a round, bare face, wearing a white button T-shirt with red lines running through it in rows and columns, and has a black trouser on.

Nigel walked back to his seat, leaving April relieved that she didn't have to hear what he had to say, although she knew what his next words were going to be, she was happy it was cut short by their teacher. She barely made it through the whole class, often present and absent at intervals, trying as much as she could to take down some notes. History has never really been her best subject, yet, she manages to pass them during tests and exams.

After class, she is at her locker getting some books out when Nigel walked up to her again. His big 6'3 inch frame towers above her 5'6 inch build. He is smiling at her again, this time, wider than before. She isn't exactly thrilled at his presence, but manages to reciprocate his smile.

"Hey, Nigel, what's up?" she says, feigning interest.

"Nothing really, I was thinking we could hang out after school? There is this big rally that will be happening in the city this afternoon, I was wondering if you would want to go?" he asks her, a hand in his pocket as he leans on one of the locker doors.

"That…would be great," April says, grinning, Nigel chortles as well, "But, I don't think I would like to be part of such a rally, I am not really a rally person," she adds, her fingers making a quotation gesture on her last words.

"Oh," he exclaims sadly, obviously dismayed at the thought of April not wanting to go to the rally with him. "But, e-everyone will be going, everyone in Daxonhill will be there, why wouldn't you want to be there?" he asks, surprised.

"Well, Nigel, not all of us are everyone. Some of us just want to go home, rest, eat, and think about the next day. Rallies do not really come to mind when you are thinking about these things," April says, shutting her locker door, and turning toward Nigel, with a reluctant look on her face.

"Okay, I thought you would want to go, you know, to drive out the nerds together."

"Not all of us see the nerds as enemies, Nigel. The sooner you realise that, the better. For now, I'm off to our next class," she said, walking past him.

"You better know that they are only about themselves, and do not see us as equals, and if you think they can be our friends, you have another thing coming," he yells, raising his voice in the hallway where he stands. April Stands still listening to him, but when he stops listening, she keeps walking, "At least, can we go get some ice cream?" he asks out loud, his hands in the air, but April doesn't stop to look back.

The alarm for dismissal rings throughout the school, and the students start to pack their stuff hurriedly to jet out of the school premises, back to their various homes or to wherever they wanted to be. April is on her way home, alone this time as Reilly was told to go home as she suddenly developed a severe stomach ache. The thoughts of Reilly keeps coming into her mind as she wonders how her friend's doing, then it goes away when she sees this couple along the road, with their child in-between them. The man is wearing a cotton overall and a black trouser, he is a bit tall, around 5'8 inches, and the woman, who seems to be the wife, has a lean figure, straight like one of those models on the front pages of magazines. She is wearing a long, flower-design velvet gown that stops right above her ankles. Their child, however, is a girl, about five years old, wearing nearly the same thing as her mum. She identifies them as one of the nerds, and decides to observe them for a while.

They walk into a restaurant located on the other side of the street, on her left. They walked in like they owned the place, their chins up and their backs straight, maintaining an upright position while walking. April could see their faces as they sat near the translucent glass of the restaurant, although not clearly due to their distance. The man and the woman sat with their backs straight, and when their little child slouched, she was told immediately to sit well, which she did smiling. Her parents were smiling at her as well. They ordered their food, and while waiting for the orders to arrive, they spoke to one another, they were having a conversation, laughing, smiling, and their child seemed to be part of it as well, as they would often turn to speak to her, and she would reply them. This seemed a little bit strange to April, "They didn't bring their phones out while they waited for their food, who doesn't press their phones while waiting for an order to come in?" she asked herself. A few moments later, their orders came in, and the man was served vegetables and beef, with a glass of wine perhaps, the woman has in her bowl, which is a white ceramic type, some salad, and also has a glass of wine too. April couldn't tell what type of drink they were having. The little girl, too, must be eating something as healthy as her parents, probably having a lot of veggies on it. April couldn't tell, the little girl was blocked by her mother's large size.

After watching them for a while, she leaves the place, and strolled home. The couple she had seen earlier couldn't stop her from thinking about her own life here in Daxonhill, about everyone's lives here in Daxonhill, how average she thinks it is compared to the lives of the smart folks, the nerds. To April, the nerds had it better, it appeared as though they had figured their lives out so well, everything was automated. And she? She was still trying to figure out how her tomorrow will be, and if it will ever be any different from what she is having now. "I guess you can't answer that until you have lived the life. A life full of misery," she said to herself, sullenly.

She gets home, and meets her mum doing the laundry.

"Good day, mum," she says to her.

"Good day, dear, how was school?" the mum inquires.

"Terrible as always," she answers, moving toward the refrigerator.

"Oh, I am sure it will get better, April dear," her mum reassures.

"Yeah, as if," she mutters, taking out a juice box of orange from the refrigerator, she pours it into a cup, and walks to the stairs, "Mum, I am going up to my room," she says, raising her voice. The mum doesn't answer.

April enters her room, and drops her bag beside a reading table, she gulps up the content in her cup, and drops it in a loud thump on the table, before walking to bed, which she jumps into. She stares into the distance for a minute, then she picks up her phone, and chats up Reilly. Reilly replies almost immediately, and April narrates how badly she had missed her in school, and Reilly promises they would hang out after school tomorrow. She also tells her about Nigel, and Reilly tells her she's too good for Nigel, that it was a good thing she didn't accept to go out with him. April lets her know that she was never going to give him a chance as she didn't consider him to have the qualities she wanted, and when Reilly asked her about such qualities, April dismissed it. Reilly tells her she has got to go, and that they would chat later, April agrees, and she drops her phone tiredly on the bed.

Then, her mind went back to the couple she had seen today, and wondered what went on in their heads, how did they think up all the things they did, was it that they possessed a type of knowledge they, the average people, didn't know of? And if they did, were they hoarding it from them? No, they couldn't. It could be us that are holding ourselves back, drawing ourselves backward, when we could be soaring as high as the smart people. But, we have decided to push them away. She thought, letting out a heavy sigh filled with frustration. And somehow, she kind of hated the nerds for not teaching them what they knew, and how to do it, they only brought their innovations, and ideas for them to purchase, though it does help them, April wanted more out of this transactional union. She spreads herself across the bedspread, imagining how it would be being a smart person, and doing things the right way, a way that would increase her value immensely.

As she lays there, her eyes to the ceiling, slowly falling asleep, she asked herself, yawning, "I wonder how it would feel being intelligent?"

CHAPTER TWO

The next day was as normal as any other days for April, nothing interesting really happened as she pulled through. On her way to school, she walked with Reilly, who seemed to be in a better state of health now, smiling as always. Her classes didn't have any tinge of excitement to them, still as listless as she had always seen them. Nigel, too, didn't seem to want to come back, but he would often give her a penetrating gaze whenever they crossed paths or in the classroom. Aside from that, her day was pretty normal.

She and Reilly are now on their way to a game shop, where they would hang out, and play some games while they are at it. It's a Friday, and this marks the beginning of a weekend both of them have always been looking forward to. A weekend of fun and leisure. April already has her weekend planned out; a lot of rest, binge-watching movies, having her favourite ice cream with peanut toppings on it, and playing loads of music till her ears bleed. The thought of it alone sends goosebumps and chills down her body, she just can't wait. For Reilly, she would be home helping her mother get ready for a wedding of a friend they would be attending. She invites April over, but she turns it down.

As they walk down the street, they see a lot of people gathered in a place, and they stop to look. It is the day sixth of the protest, and someone is on a podium addressing the large crowd before him, he is holding a megaphone right up to his mouth, speaking into it. The man has a brown skin like cocoa-butter, a short hair, and has an electronic voice due to the megaphone he's speaking into. April and Reilly could hear what he is saying, and while nods in agreement, April, however, is indifferent to everything. The man's "We are tired of living like slaves to these people that they have all the answers to everything. We are tired of taking instructions from them, and doing what they recommend. We are tired of them making us feel we are not enough, like we are some children they can tell what to do. And it's their children that needs to be told what to do, those kids be acting like some things are above them, acting all uppity, speaking back at their seniors. I say enough is enough!" had no impression on April, as she thinks such an outburst was uncalled for, but Reilly seems to be enjoying the man's speech, as she lets out a loud "Yes," which made April turn to her in bewilderment.

She looks back at the crowd, and she sees the kind of people there, people she thinks may need a little help from these so-called 'supercilious' folks. Her eyes fell on a girl with a lot of make-up, and wondered how much make-up can someone need. She spots a bodybuilder who might have taken his bodybuilding way too far, as his bulging muscles fit into a shirt that may be large enough to pass as a short dress for her. She also sees a man with his beer in hand, he has a protruding stomach, a shabby look, and wears a white shirt with stain marks on it, which doesn't seem to fit well on him as his bulging stomach is left open. She also sees a mother clutching her crying baby in hand, under the sun's heat, she is trying as best as she could to stop the baby from crying. She sees other people, and thinks they should be in other places but here.

"Don't you want to go to the game store anymore? Or, would you rather stay here?" April asks.

"Oh, yeah, I almost forgot," replies Reilly with a smile.

They walked in silence for a while, Reilly's hands in her baggy jean trousers, and April trying to walk like the couple she saw the day before. Reilly kept on looking at her as though she had something to tell her, April noticed, and wondered what was on her mind.

"What is it?" April asks, looking at her.

"What is what?" Reilly replies.

"You have been acting as though there's something bothering you, and you want to lay it off your chest, so I am asking, what is it?"

"Nothing really, just that I have been thinking, why is it that you are not as involved as everyone else when it comes to the nerds? Like, obviously we can see how these people behave, and act like their lives are perfect, don't you see this all?"

April stays mute for a while, thinking of an answer. She agrees that they might be acting all 'high modern,' and they did things differently from them in Daxonhill. But compared to their town, Anthera coast was a heaven of good living, with their classy and glassy skyscrapers, their organized roads and streetlights, their wonderful architecture, and Roman-styled buildings, the abundance of food and clean water. All this makes April rethink her position on the hate on nerds.

"Well, aren't you going to say anything?" Reilly asks, jostling her back to reality.

Startled, she looks around, and realised they have been walking for a while, and they were about to approach the games store.

"Well, we are here," April says, grinning.

"April!" Reilly calls out, not exactly pleased with April's defiance.

***

Inside the games store, they help themselves to a handful of arcade games; Mario world, Monkey kong, Ping-pong man, and rode a motorcycle with a virtual reality screen. They are having fun as they talk about everything that isn't about the nerds or the protest outside, April had made sure of that. Now, they just play, and try to beat one another. During their games, Reilly doesn't seem to be having much luck on them, April keeps on winning, and scoring more points than she ever could, and she starts to think where she learned to play so well.

"You never mentioned you knew how to play this good?" she asks, trying frantically to beat April in an aim-and-shoot game.

"Well, I was tired of my brother, and you beating me in every game we played back in the day, I was tired of losing, and so I would often come out here on my own, and learn," she confesses, "Yes!" she exclaims happily, jumping into the air.

"Seems like I have some catching up to do then," says Reilly.

"Yes, you do."

Meanwhile, on the other side of the store, are some guys who have been glancing and making remarks on the two girls, and whenever they felt someone was watching them, they would turn. The boys would quickly turn away to avoid detection. A minute later, one of the boys makes to walk over to the girls, but he is held back by the others, but this doesn't deter him. He gets free from them, and walks up to April and Reilly. Slowly, his 6 inch build comes closer to the girls, and soon, he is standing before them, smiling.

"Good day, ladies," he says to them.

They turn to meet him, replying, "Good day," giving him a cursory look, before making to leave.

He glances toward the screen, and turns to them again, "I see you are the one with the most score here, for the fifth time in a row, miss April," he says, talking to April, "It's April, right? At least, it says here 'April' with your score next to it," he adds.

April turns to him as well, refusing to be dragged away by Reilly, "Yes, that me. It wasn't easy beating the last person who scored the highest on the game, I think it was written KLY or something, can't remember," she let him know.

"Oh, well, I am in a bit of a mood to play, maybe I might knock you out of your place in the game's leaderboard, who knows. But, I must warn you, I shoot very well," he says with a daring glare, handing her a shooter.

April scoffs, "You wish,"

"Would you care to indulge me?" he asks.

"I can't believe we are doing this right now," says Reilly, bemused. She grabs April to the side, "Don't you know who he is? He's one of them" she says in hush tones, looking at the guy standing in waiting for April.

"Of course, I do. it was pretty obvious from the beginning." she replies in hush tones.

"And you are going to play with him? To indulge him or whatever that word meant," Reilly tells her, her face a canvass of disgust and worry.

"Relax, he is only a nerd, and nothing more," she says, walking toward him again, "Let's play," she says to him.

He smiles, and hands her the game shooter. She takes it, and they position themselves to play. Reilly is on the other side, with her lips lowered in frustration, she looks over to the other guys where their friend came from, and looks away quickly when one of them waved at her, she wasn't about to frolick with any guy from the seaside city of Anthera. She can't! She thought to herself. April and the stranger have started playing their game, shooting away at the screen as they shoot to pieces as much fruit as they can in the shortest amount of time, shooting down bonuses as well. April is highly focused on the game, and feels uneasy as she feels her game partner is following closely behind her in scores, shortly, he passes her, and this plunges her into a state of anxiety. She tries vigorously to pass him, but it's not working, and she begins to panic. Her game partner notices this when he turns to see her, but continues to play. He wears a determined expression, and shoots as fast as he can. Suddenly, April starts to take the lead, she sees this, and her heart stops heaving, and the gathered beads of sweat on her forehead start to dry up. She looks up to the man beside her, and finds him stern-faced, she feels happy because she thinks her winning is getting to him, and this only makes her play even harder. At the end, April wins yet again.

"Yes!" she screams in excitement.

Reilly stands upright, and smiles broadly, seeing her friend beat a nerd. "That's my girl, April!" she says out loud.

He sighs, and turns to her with a smile, "Seems like I could beat you, and for this, I congratulate you on your win, miss April," he says.

"Thank you, mister…"

"Call me Kelly," he says.

"Kelly," she said, "Thank you for your words."

"You are most certainly welcome. Although, I did wish I could have scored higher this time on Fruit martial, would have been good."

"This time? Have you ever played before?"

"Yes, although it's been some years I haven't played it. I considered it small for my taste as I advanced in my gaming skills. I had a high score that no one could beat for a long time."

"Oh," she let out, thinking, "A score no one could beat? You said your name is Kelly, right?"

"That's very correct."

"And you have played Fruit martial, which means that high score I spent nearly a year trying to beat was yours? That means, you are KLY?"

He lets out a chuckle, "That's right, miss April. And, it's a wonderful thing to see someone as wily as you could break it," he says.

"Is that supposed to be a compliment or what?" she asks with a wry face.

"It's a compliment," he says in defense, "Please, do not be offended," he adds.

"I am not, I guess," she says, turning to Reilly, who is now walking up to her.

"Well, it was fun playing with you, Kelly, but I must go now. As you can see, my friend is already here."

"It is alright, miss April, but I believe we should be crossing paths again soon, am I right?"

"No, you won't," said Reilly in a haughty tone, dragging April behind her, "We are done here."

He looks at them as they walk out of the section where he is, "Will I see you again?" he asks, almost screaming.

"I don't think so," April shouts over her shoulders.

Her reply dampens his mood, as he walks wearily back to his friends, all four of them, who are waiting in anticipation to what he has got to say to them. He gets to them, and takes his seat.

"Well, that didn't seem to go well," a friend of his says to him. He is a guy with a pale face, and dark brown hair, slightly brown eyebrows, and dark eyes.

"It went as south as we said it would. We told you, these Daxonhill girls do not possess the intuition to know quality guys when they are approached by one," another with a ponytail, and jet grey eyes says.

Kelly looks up at him, "I have she will come around," he said to him, sipping on a smoothie on the table.

"Do not say I didn't warn you, that we didn't warn you. When all this comes crashing, maybe then, you will realise your mistake. Besides, aren't you supposed to be at a physical wellness class right this moment?" the friend says.

"I skipped it," Kelly replies.

All four of them gasped.

"I see you are not taking your health very seriously, Kelly, your father will not be pleased at such an aberration, you know that?"

"I am certain he wouldn't mind, trust me. He lets me go however I please," he says with a boastful look on his face.

"And, what if she doesn't like you, kelly?" the brown haired guy asks.

"Simple, I will make her like me."

His friend narrows his eyes, and lets out a sigh, "You do know we are hated here, right? That we aren't accepted? Everyone hates us.".

"If that's the case, I will try and blend in, maybe that might pique her interest in me. For, just as Bismarck said 'If you are in Rome, act like the Romans,' there's wisdom there, my friends," he tells them, a smug smile on his face.

CHAPTER THREE

On the bus home, Reilly couldn't keep her mouth closed for a minute, couldn't help herself to stop talking about the nerd they had met earlier. She kept on making remarks about him, and his friends that sat watching them while they were at the game control station, and most of these remarks were words that made April's head hurt a bit and her eyes glancing now and again at Reilly. She couldn't take it anymore, and how she had tried to make Reilly's voice a muffled tone. Alas, she couldn't take it.

"Reilly!" she shouts, "Can you please keep it quiet till we get to my place," April demands, slumping into her seat furiously.

Reilly froze to a stop, a puzzled look on her face. She said nothing, and April said nothing too—she had nothing much to say. Her mind was also not at ease, and it wasn't for the same reasons as Reilly's.

However, they had arrived home over thirty minutes ago, and are now in April's room. Reilly had a tensed look on her face, and has been looking at April's uninterested face as she scrolls through her phone.

April knows Reilly has something in mind, a thought that's pricking her so bad she might explode any minute.

This makes her feel conflicted inside, contemplating if she should let Reilly speak out her thoughts or remain in ignorance to it. Though, it's not much of an ignorance if she already knows what it is.

She steals a quick look at Reilly, then back at her phone. She says to herself, 'If I ask her what's she thinking of, she will talk about nothing else but the nerd from earlier. Can't she just let it rest?'

She sighs.

Reilly sighs too. She turns her gaze toward April, who's still looking through her phone, she grunts depressingly, then pulls out her phone as well.

"What is it, Reilly?" April asks, tired of the sickening silence between them.

Reilly looks at her with a feigned, flushed expression, "Oh, sorry, I didn't know you would still want to talk. I thought you were avoiding me."

"I would have loved to, but your…movements were too noisy."

"I was literally not making any noise."

"Exactly what I am saying."

Both of them pause, staring into their thoughtful faces — April's that of vexation and Reilly's that of bemusement, both their bodies heaving as they thought of what next to say.

April relaxes, she asks with a soft air to her voice, "What is wrong, Reilly?"

Reilly sighs, her gaze across the room, "You know what's on mind, April, you know it."

"Please, do not tell me it's because–"

"It's because of them of course, April! Because of him!" Reilly interjects quickly.

"What about him? I haven't seen anything wrong that he had done, or was talking to me a crime?"

Reilly scoffs, her face folds with bewilderment, "How can you say that, April? These are people our society is trying to kick out, didn't you see how gloated they were, how they took pride in what they did?"

April takes her eyes away from her phone for a moment, looking distinctively into space, her mind trying to see the light and meaning in her friend's words.

She shrugs, "I didn't see anything. They acted pretty normal to me, like how boys should act. Normal boys, that is."

Reilly furrows her brows, she scoffs again at April's words, thinking how outrageous and outlandish her statement was. Is April really making this statement? When had she suddenly turned cold toward matters that had to do with the nerds and what they did to them.

April, for the best years Reilly had known her, had been her friend, wasn't this way. She remembered her to be quite vocal and outward in her views about the nerds, sharing the same thoughts with her and joining her to condemn them. But, as she stares at the pale face scrolling through her phone, she no longer sees the April that would call out the smart people for the injustice; the April that could challenge a nerd even though she will be beaten intellectually, she no longer sees that April. All she sees now is a shadow of her, a carcass empty of life and vigor, and the spirit needed to do what their society upholds. That April is gone, and she knows it.

"Is that all you can say, huh?" she asks.

"It is not that serious, and even if it is, I don't see why you should be stressing over it. Yes, I know you don't like how they may behave at times, or the way they speak and laugh, or eat their food, but a guy speaking to me shouldn't be something you should get all worked up about."

Reilly stays mute, her eyes filled with questions. She seems to be seeing the logic in April's words, the sense in it. And as she takes her gaze toward the left corner of April's room, her mind begins to connect the dots, making sense of it all.

She slumps into April's bed, "I still think they are no good."
April rolls her eyes, she murmurs, "That's for you to say."

"What did you say?"

"Nothing."

Reilly relaxes back into the bed. She is still wearing a thoughtful expression on her face, as though about to say something else.

"I never told you about what happened to me yesterday," she says suddenly, "And I just remembered that you didn't even care to ask, you didn't even ask me all throughout today. My God!"

April is stunned, she apologizes, "It is not what you think, Reilly. I meant to ask you, I really did, believe me."

Reilly stares at her for a moment, she shrugs, "I believe you. I know you would have asked if you had remembered. It's alright."

April's body sinks in a sigh, a sigh of relief, "Thank you … So, what happened to you yesterday that you had to go home so early?"

"Yeah…remember the time I told you I had been hungry these days, and tired and thirsty, and… I cannot remember the last one, but you remember, right?"

April turns toward Reilly with a worried look on her face, "Yes, I do. What's wrong?"

"Yeah, turns out I have diabetes." Reilly says in a hush, sad tone.

April's face falls to Reilly's hands, they are almost shaking as she fiddles with them. April could feel Reilly's pulsating heart, the wrecking to her nerve, and the tightening in her chest. The silence between them makes April even more anxious, she searches her face and the weariness in those pale eyes were more outspoken than any word Reilly could ever utter.

"I am sorry to hear that, Reilly," she says softly.

Reilly nods her head in self-pity, "It's alright, April. I mean, who doesn't have diabetes, or who hasn't gotten it before? Certainly, I am not the first person, and won't be the last either."

"That is true," she says, dropping her phone on the bed, "I can only imagine what you are going through."

Reilly waves her hand in the air, treating the matter lightly, "Nahh, it's not that bad, trust me. Yes, I may need to be visiting the doctor now and again, take something called insulin, exercise, lose weight–"

"Lose weight?" April asks with a perplexed face, "You don't look like you need to lose weight?" she chuckles.

"Exactly what I told them!" Reilly exclaims, "But, they said it is necessary for me if I am to keep my blood sugar levels stable," she says mockingly.

"Well, I guess they mean well for you then, and want you alive too."

Reilly falls into the bed, "Whatever. I just hate the fact I won't be able to eat what I want anymore."

A thought flashes through April's face, "Speaking of eating, are you hungry? You must be because I am starving right now."

"Yes, please. Do bring some food for us, I am quite hungry too."

April gets out of bed and into the hallway that leads downstairs, and in minutes, she comes back with a plate of pizza and two cups of drinks saddled on a tray.

Reilly pulls herself upright, "That was fast, did you warp time or something? Where did you get a pizza from?"

She walks toward Reilly and places the tray on the sheets, "Woah, that's a lot of questions, girl. But, first off, I didn't waste time. I wish I could, but I didn't. I only got the pizza from the fridge and microwaved it for a small amount of time, quick enough to heat it up, and brought it here, for us. And I guess I have already answered the second question."

Reilly shoots her a smile, moving in to pick up a piece of pizza, "It's alright, though I hope this doesn't kill me later."

April stops midway into eating her pizza, her stunned eyes on Reilly's face, "Why is that? Is the pizza bad for you?"

Reilly bites into the baked, triangle dough, speaking as she ate, "Kind of, I guess. The doctors said too much carbs can affect my sugar levels and can lead to tiredness, weight loss, blurred vision, skin infection, and some other infections like thrush and cystitis, and some other stuff I can't seem to remember."

April doesn't say anything for a minute, her face rapt with attention, but it all soon falls and forms into a sly smile, one which made Reilly look at her queerly.

"Why is your face like that?" Reilly asls with an arched brow.

"You know what? You are starting to sound like a nerd right now, with the way you are explaining your sickness," she starts laughing.

"Oh, come on now, April, I still hate them." She says picking up another piece.

This throws April into a bout of laughter, her pizza still in mouth and with not a care in the world what Reilly thinks. She tries covering her mouth, but her cackling won't let her. She would fall on her right and then, on her left, her laughs bouncing off the walls of her blue walled room, causing Reilly to eat with rising debasing feelings as April mocks her with her laugh.

But as April laughed, she realized there may be more to being a nerd than she had thought.

***

The time is half past 7:00 PM, April's family are getting the table ready for dinner. And, as it has been done for ages now, about 16 years anyways, April and her mom, Dareen, are the ones to cook the food and set the table. April would handle the table and her mother, the cooking. Dareen has always had her reservations about April doing the cooking, she believes her daughter will make a mess of things, even though April can hold her own forte in the kitchen.

In the dining room, dimly lit by a brown light above, an oak table is placed in the centre of it, with six chairs made of the same material—oak— surrounding the triangle-shaped, brown wood. Two chairs have been reserved by the family for guests, just in case one or two persons decide to pop into the house and say hello.

With keen eyes and attention to what she is doing, April

lays the plates and utensils where they should all be. White ceramic plates placed before each chair, with silver forks and knives placed on both sides of the plates. Accompanying these plates are glass cups meant for whatever liquid they will be having that night.

She wasn't thinking much this time, as soon as Reilly left, she slipped into her bed and caught a quick sleep, only to be woken up moments later to come help out down in the kitchen. Her ears were blocked shut by two, white earbuds that sent pop music into her eardrums, bouncing off them with a reverberating beat and a rhythm that sends April bumping her head to every chord.

Her tiny, colorful flare of sounds is soon disturbed as Damien taps her on the side, an attempt to get her attention.

She takes off an earbud, her furious eyes slapped on Damien's face, "What?"

"Why aren't you helping mom in the kitchen?" he asks, taking a seat on one of the chairs.

"Mom doesn't want me there this time, she said she can handle the cooking herself."

"Oh. That's mom for you, always the superwoman who is needed in the house."

"Yeah."

April takes out her earbud case and sinks the one she had removed into it, as she has realized Damien is here to chat with her. Talking with her little brother has always been a pleasure for April. She loves the way he makes jokes out of things. His understanding of various issues that ought to be a bit complex often has a way to make her second guess who is really talking to. He is always a pad to have around, and she loves it when they have a little conversation.

She is done setting the table, a satisfied look flushing through her face as she glares at the rightly placed dining sets she had arranged. She sighs a breath and turns to leave.

Damien doesn't seem to be in the mood to talk. He was fiddling with his fingers when he saw April walking toward the kitchen door. He swallows, and makes to speak.

"Your friend, Reilly," he says to April, stopping her in her steps.

April searches her mind for a possible reason for Damien's statement, darting her eyes here and there. She asks as she couldn't get any, "Yes? What about her?"

"I saw her leave the house this afternoon, on my way home from school," he says nervously.

April starts to get a sense of what he is saying, or where he is driving at. She walks closer to Damien, slowly, with a bemused grin on her face.

"Okay? What happened?"

Damien maintains a hold of April's flaring gaze, his lips rising in a nervous smile, "I think she has a beautiful smile."

April lets her body fall, relaxing with a wider grin on her face. Wider and more wholesome than it should have been. However, she was expecting such a statement from her brother, and knew she wouldn't be all that surprised about him having a crush on her friend, Reilly.

"Aww, I see that someone's feelings are getting the best of him," she says, poking him with her fingers.

Damien pushes her hands away, with a blush on his face, "Stop it. I was only saying, you don't have to make it look like I have something for her."

She pauses, looking at her brother with searching eyes, "But, you do."

"No, I don't."

She turns to leave, "Any which way, get over it, she's too old for you."

April's words hit him cold, like a bucket of ice cubes being poured on him on a cold afternoon. He watches his sister leave his side with a faint smile on her face, his heart beating faster and faster, Damien shrivels his face and looks away. A slight burning has eased up into his chest, and he hated it.

"Age doesn't matter, you know!"

"Not when you are 12, it doesn't."

Damien slumps into the chair, furious and agitated.

A few minutes later, plates were filled with the evening meal Dareen had prepared, rice with cooked corn and slices of beef, and their cups filled with water. Everyone are busy with their meals, Morris and Dareen are giving each other suggestive, piercing glances; Damien is eating with a bitterness in his mouth, though he knows his mother's cooking is good, he still feels a stale taste to his tongue; April has her earbuds in her ears, shutting out her family out the best way she can.

Morris glances at Dareen again, she returns the look, holding it as they eat. She gives him a nod, as though telling him to go ahead with something. He clears his throat, "Errm, can I have everyone's attention, please?"

All eyes soon turn toward the round, bare face with dark brown hair. He has a smile on his face, one of anxiety and excitement, his grin getting wider and wider the more he stays quiet, watching the expectant gazes of his family. Morris doesn't seem to be able to say anything, he has been gripped with a dreadful feeling, and his tongue can't seem to want to say a word. He swallows again and again, makes to say, yet nothing.

"Well, children," Dareen calls the attention of April and Damien, "Your father has something important he would like to share with us. Just give him a little time, I am sure he will say it."

They revert their gazes from their mother back to their father, watching him as he steadies himself.

"Yes, err… I will like to let you know that I will be asking for a promotion. Instead of working as a…regular office staff, doing mere paperwork, I was thinking of taking it a step higher, you know…seeking a role higher than my current position."

They all glance at each other, eyes moving from one puzzled face to the other. Dareen is wearing an uneasy smile, and her eyes seem to be twitching more often than she can notice. She is just as nervous as her husband, nervous of what the children might think of his move.

"Wow, dad, that's great." Damien congratulates him, "Finally, you are about to show them how it's done."

Morris lets out a content smile, he feels a lesser pressure now in his chest. Someone seems to have the same thought as him—his son with a lighter brown to his hair. He turns his gaze to April, who has her head buried in her food.

April could feel the stares of her parents as it bores down on her, their almost silent eyes piercing into her body like little, sharp needles or a wet, clammy hand rubbing itself against her skin. She doesn't want to say anything, she knows they wouldn't like it, so why say it? She gives her father a side glance and takes it back the moment she sees him watching, chills running down her body.

She passes a tongue through her dry lips, deciding against her thought of not saying a word.

"So, what role are you going for, dad?" she says finally.

Morris beams at her, then at Dareen, "Oh, ahh…it's a managerial role, a senior product manager. It comes with a good pay raise too."

"Huh, that's nice," she says with a fake grin, nodding her head approvingly at her father, "My only hope is you get the job done the way you should."

Morris' face turned into a dull sheet of eyes and nose and mouth, the colors that were once there had all disappeared, making April resent her earlier statement.

"Of course, I can handle the job, what do you take me for? A half-wit?"

"Dad, no. That's not what I meant," she says in her defense, "It's just that, the nerds–"

"It isn't always about the nerds, April. Even if we can do what they can, all we need is a chance, just a chance."

April stares at the fearful, brown eyes of her father, she could see how uncertain he is, yet wanting to prove that he is able at a particular thing. She is happy for him, but she's worried. Worried that he may not meet up, and at the end, a mockery will be made out of him.

She says nothing as she continues to eat her meal. Everyone else stays silent, causing the air to be filled with a mist of frigid feelings loud enough to be heard.

However, April knew she had a point.

CHAPTER FOUR

April's mood has been melancholic since yesterday, having to say those words to her dad and seeing the hurt on his face made her feel a tight knot in her belly, a retching she can't seem to think away.

But, during that moment, she hadn't meant it, her statement about her father's competence and capability. She hadn't wanted her father to feel sad, or have him see her as a pessimist, but she felt this was one of the things she couldn't control fully in her life.

This morning as she got ready for school, she apologized to her dad, her heart pumping faster and faster as she did it. She didn't want a moment to pass and her father is still bothered by her words of yesterday, and so, as she was getting milk out of the fridge, seeing her father coming into the kitchen area, she told him how sorry she was.

"It's okay, April. I know you said it from a place of care. I understand." He said with a soft smile.

April wasn't convinced, she took some steps closer to him, "Are you sure? I mean, I can't imagine you being hurt, I only just want to make sure."

"Really, April, I'm good," he said, "I have already decided to go for the role, and that's that, not even your words can stop that. So, I am fine," he said, placing a hand on April's shoulder.

A warm, apologetic smile beamed at him, her eyes more remorseful than it had ever been. She watched as her father got the thing he wanted, a drink of water, and walked away. She sighed.

That moment brought a feeling of relief to the retching inside of her, and she could finally go to school with a saner state of mind.

April had just finished from a class, and is now at her locker, taking out some notes for her next class. She has earbuds on as her school, Daxonhill High, allows students to have their gadgets around as opposed to how the nerds did theirs. They never really conform to what the nerds do, and so, their lives were a little different from them.

Music blasting at mid volume, April bumping her head to it, her expression is lot lighter than before. She takes out her books, and set to close her locker when she feels two hands clasp her shoulders, and a faint noise is heard. She turns, with a bewildered mien, to see who has decided to play tricks with her. It is Reilly. All smiles and white, sturdy teeth gleaming under the hallway lights.

She takes out her earbuds, which were under the green woolen cap on her head, she asks, "Reilly, where were you this morning?"

Reilly asks with her hyper voice, "You have got to be kidding me, you had earbuds on?"

"Of course, I have earbuds on. How do you expect me to keep breathing in this school?" she asks rhetorically.

Reilly with an arched brow, replies, "That's true. This school is torture. Some days, I don't even feel like coming, and yet, Monday to Friday, I am here for straight 7 hours."

"Hmm," she makes a close-lip sound with a disinterested face, "So, why weren't you in school early this morning? I didn't see you in class."

Reilly pushes some hair away from her face, adjusting her backpack firmly on her shoulder, she replies, "Yes, I had to stay home for a while as I had felt a bit wonky this morning. My parents even suggested I stay home for today, but I told them they shouldn't bother, I could still make it to school. So, when I started feeling better, I came here, to this prison."

"Oh, so sorry to hear that," she sympathized, "Was it because of your health?"

Reilly nods happily, "I guess I ate too much carbs yesterday, which was why I felt a little sick this morning. But, it all worked out fine in the end, after I took an insulin injection, I was okay again. See?"

Reilly was more lively than she had ever been, her mood seems as though she didn't want anything to dull it or her spirit. She was joyous. She looked strong and boisterous, as though she hadn't hated her worst enemies – the nerds.

But, beneath all that smile and chatter, and her glowing, bright eyes, April felt what Reilly doesn't want to show. And she was glad her friend wanted it that way. Inside her, April smiled, and she thought how strong her friend is.

"Yes, Reilly, I can see that."

They stay beaming at each other with a smile, their eyes like stars in the night sky, full of warmth and care. Reilly is even more content that she needn't explain much about her health, or act like it is a death sentence, because, frankly, she knows there's more to life than worrying over something she knew could be controlled. And, if she ever needed help managing her health, she knows she has got a friend who will be there.

Reilly sighs, "So, when is our next class?"

April looks at her with a befuddled eye, "Don't tell me you have–"

"Hey," a near bass voice said.

The two girls turn their gaze toward the voice, their eyes soon coming in contact with a black haired guy with a bare face, a square chin and an athletic build. He is wearing a grey T-shirt underneath another shirt with its buttons undone and a pair of cream-colored pants. He has his backpack saddled to one his shoulders, shooting the two girls the best smile he could put up.

"Hey, Nigel, how are you doing?" Reilly asks him with a wide, flirtatious smile.

"I am good, Reilly," he says to her, then he turns his gaze to April, who has her eyes on Reilly, "Hello, April, I see you're ready for class." Nigel says nervously.

"Uhh, yes, but there's still time, so I was just thinking of going to the class to wait," she says, turning to Reilly, hoping she caught on. But, she didn't, "Isn't that so, Reilly?"

Reilly turns to her in surprise, "No, we didn't discuss that. When did we discuss that?"

April couldn't believe her friend would do such a thing to her, something as simple as acting in line with her thoughts. She had given the eyes, the jerk of her brows, the tugging of Reilly's sweater, yet, Reilly couldn't pick up the message, and this made her curse inside.

She sucks it up, and awaits what Nigel has to say. She shoots him a feigned, wide grin, the sides of her cheeks and eyes folding as a result of the forced smile. Nigel smiles back, letting out a soft but nervous chuckle.

"So, Nigel, what have you been up to lately?" Reilly asks, poking him playfully with her middle finger.

"Uhh, nothing much, really. I am only here to speak with April, that's all."

Reilly makes a false grimace of her being surprised by Nigel wanting to talk to April. She turns to her and April shrugs the thought away. Then, she turns back to Nigel with not a word to say but an awkward smile.

"Huh, April?" he calls her, "I was thinking, about the last time we spoke, I later realized that I might have made you mad, and I would like to apologize for that. Please, can you forgive me?"

April stares at him with an indifferent look on her face,

she could see how resentful he looks and Nigel is supposed to be counted as one of the toughest guys in the school. No one dared to get him angry or pick a fight with him, he had his friends who were also tough, and being one of those in the football team, he is also respected.

Now, here he is, like a puppy who had gone astray and had just found its mother, asking April for an apology. This, too, sent roving thoughts through Reilly. Okay, this is new, says Reilly.

She exhales, hesitating to speak, "Yeah, it's fine, Nigel. No need to apologize, I wasn't offended, really."

She waves her hand in the air, adjusting the strap of her bag around her shoulder. She feels a bit odd toward everything as she had already forgotten about Nigel's remarks about the nerds, though a lurch had appeared in her stomach that day, she no longer felt weary about it. It is now in the past, why would he bring it up again, she thinks.

Nigel nods, then turns to Reilly, "I guess I will be seeing you two later then."

"Yeah, you surely will." Reilly tells him with an overt smile. So overt, it made him a bit uncomfortable as he walked away.

"Bye, Nigel," says Reilly. She follows him with her eyes before fixing them on April, "What was that all about?"

"It was just a little argument we had, it's nothing. Let's go to class," she says, walking forward with Reilly following behind.

"Okay. Well, it's good both of you have settled now, I wouldn't want that smooth face of his to be wrinkled over you."

April arches her brow at her smiling friend, "Okay, whatever you say."

She shakes her head to the thought of Reilly having a crush on Nigel, and she hasn't even told her yet. Reilly is supposed to be her best friend, and she keeping such a thing from her irked her in a way. But, April waves it off anyway, she knows Reilly will let her know about her feelings for him someday, she will wait for it.

***

In the class, everyone is waiting for the teacher to come in, but not in the typical, good student manner. The class is rowdy, full of chatter, full of life, the students' voices rise high into the ceiling, seeping into the walls and out into the hallway. Some are running around, some are sitting, but mostly, almost everyone is talking, with voices so loud it can swallow another's. Hence, the reason for their raised voices

Unlike every other student in the noisy class, April sits on her chair, patiently waiting for the teacher to come. She anticipates the teacher's class, she likes the man and the way he teaches. He teaches life sciences, explaining to them how the planet earth works and thrives, with all its complexities. April considers him a nerd worth learning from, and would tell of other students who dared to challenge him. But then, she also anticipates the closure of school, so they can go home.

A few moments later, A man in a red and white striped

shirt walks into the class. The shirt is tucked into his brown trouser, despite his protruding belly. He has dark hair and a dark mustache, he also has benign, dark eyes, and an almost permanent faint smile on his plump, round, bearded face. Something April likes too. The teacher is Mr. Arnav

His presence brought a cover of silence to befall the class, as students scampered to their various seats. He still has his smile on him, watching as the students behave.

"Alright now," Mr. Arnav said, a word he seems to love saying very much, "Good morning, students."

"Good morning, sir," responds only a few students, including April. The rest of the class were quiet.

Mr. Arnav exhales a breath, the side of his lips still raised in a faint smile, almost smuggish in a way, "I will say it again, and I hope I get those who will receive points for being good students."

"We don't need your points," screams one of the students.

April turns to see this person, her disgusted eyes soon fall on a boy with orange hair, and fleshy face with stubby nose. She rolls her eyes and sits back in her position.

"You might not need it, but I am doing all in my capability to show you that there's reward in being good. If you don't see that, then the society we live in will not be safe for you and me. Even you will hate it, and trust me, you don't want that." He says to the boy.

Their eyes are on him, their tongues tied, ruminating on

what he has just said. He has a point, but their elusive realities wouldn't let some of them see or think clearly. When Mr. Arnav saw there was no more protest, he took a breath and makes to speak.

"Good morning once again, everyone."

"Good morning, sir." They respond, though their voices were uneven in sounds.

Mr. Arnav smiles, satisfied with the result he has gotten. A content eye peering at every students' face. He is a teacher, he is already used to their disinterested expressions. Besides, this is Daxonhill.

"Now, can anyone tell me what we did last time? Anyone?" he asks them, stepping in front of the class.

The class goes quiet, like always. He had been expecting this, he always did. Yet, everytime he comes in to teach, he would always ask them the question, it was a way he had devised to get them thinking and latching onto his words anytime he starts talking. He doesn't bother them much, because he knows a lot of the students don't like him, yet, they pass his class. Which he likes.

"So, no one can tell me what we had done in our previous class?" he asks, sounding surprised.

Yet, no one answered, only penetrating stares came his way. April felt an urge to raise her hand and speak, but her legs gave way to numbness in this type of situation. Her anxiety wouldn't let her, even though she knows the answer.

"Alright then, since no one will say anything, we shall

continue with our next topic. This is an offshoot from the last topic, so we are not really trailing off that much," he tells them, walking back to the chalk, "Please, take out your pen and paper, and listen carefully. This one will be interesting."

Excitedly, April digs into her bag which she had looped around her chair. She gets out what she needed, and readied herself for the lecture. Other students, however, did their lazily, groaning and complaining silently, and April wonders why they couldn't be as excited as she is, though she doesn't make it open.

Mr. Arnav then goes on to discuss with the class prehistoric creatures. He had done that during the last class, but on dinosaurs. That had fascinated most of the class, with April being the most attentive during it. Talking about animals that had once existed millions of years ago had a way of imprinting itself into their minds, picturing what it was like for these creatures to exist, to feed and survive in their various habitats. This made every travel beyond the class, making it quiet and somewhat interactive. Mr. Arnav felt wholesome after his lecture.

During this time, his lecture is on prehistoric animals that lived after the extinction of the dinosaurs – the mammoths, the megalodons, the silver-tooth cats of the stone ages. As he speaks to the class about these creatures and how they cohabited with the humans of that time, he paced the class, making sure all heard him.

"The sabre-tooth cats were the biggest of all cats during the stone age, much bigger than the biggest cat we have now. They had long teeth on both sides of their upper jaws, protruding when their mouths are closed. And their claws were sharp enough to tear down the toughest creature that ever existed during that time. They existed 16 million years ago, and with two known families like the smilodon and the machairodont." He tells them, gesturing with his hands.

As he walks back and forth the class, in slow and measured steps, April's ears are rapt with interest, holding onto every word Mr. Arnav is saying. And when the time for the end of the lecture started to draw near, April wishes he could continue a little bit, but her teacher is a very disciplined man.

"And, therefore, the megalodons were unrivaled in the sea, even being able to tear through the biggest whales that existed then. And the whales then were also very massive," he tells them, with glee in his eyes, "Now, any questions?"

The students stare curiously at him, none of them making an attempt to say anything. Mr. Arnav runs his eyes through the rooms, looking into the faces that stared back at him. Some avoided his gaze, and some didn't, and when he made to say something, someone raises up a hand.

"Sir?" a female voice says as Mr. Arnav's eyes fall on her. It is April.

He gestures to her to speak, and shyly, looking around her to see the eyes that bogged down on her, she makes to speak, albeit gripped with anxiety.

"Why did most of the animals then disappear, only to change into smaller versions of themselves now? Why didn't they remain as they were then?" April asks, her voice almost inaudible and husky. She shrinks back into her chair after she has asked her question.

Mr. Arnav smiles, walking away from his table, "You see, various situations on our earth can cause us to evolve, to change from one form or appearance to another. Before now, we humans weren't this way, we were sturdier, more stubby, and a lot less good looking. We were quite ugly."

The class laughs at his last statement, gladdening him.

He continues, "But, as time went on, and we started to migrate or adapt to various conditions, our bodies started to undergo change, so it can survive in that condition. The same applies to animals too. This happens through a process called natural selection, where a gene or trait is passed down from one specie to its offsprings, giving it that same trait or features. And another is mutation, as animals can change their features to fit a particular climatic condition.

In the case of the prehistoric animals or men, climate and geological migration were an integral part in their evolution. As their climate changed, and their environment changed, these animals, no matter how strong they were, had to change with it. The ones that couldn't, died, bringing forth new species. And, millions of years later, we are here, evolved and still evolving."

As Mr. Arnav was explaining, the class listened with heightened attention, all eyes were on him, and their minds helped them picture various moments in time when things changed. Hence, the reason why they love the class so much. Mr. Arnav walks back to his desk, and with a sigh of content, he places his hands on the desk gently, looking into the students' faces.

"And, that's out of the way, I would like to give you all a project to take home," he tells them, but it didn't meet most of the students well, "Now-now, I know how you all dread class projects, but trust me, this one will be fun."

"For you, right?!" a student bellows.

"No," replies Mr. Arnav calmly, "It's for you. For all of you, and trust me, this will help you all cooperate better, sharing ideas with one another like a team. Don't you want that?"

"No!" they chorused noisily, defiant in manner.

"Well, it has already been decided, and your names have been paired up already," he tells them, reaching for an item under his desk. He brings it up, and drops it on the desk, "Alright now, each group is allowed to choose a topic they want or like, and research on it. It can be anything, so long it's on our subject, the prehistoric times and creatures, including man himself. In this box is the list of names that have been paired, put into a group of two. It has been on a small sheet of paper, so come forward and check your names. The project should be submitted in the next three weeks, so get it ready before then. I will see you all in our next class. Good luck, you all." Mr. Arnav tells them, taking his leave out of the class.

As Mr. Arnav leaves the class, Reilly and April glance at each other. Horror and excitement fill their eyes, their mind thinking the same thing. April gets to her feet, and walls up to where Reilly is sitting. Reilly stands up too, smiling and gripped with anxiety of the unknown. She gasps as April comes closer.

"Want to check it out?" April asks.

Reilly looks toward the teacher's desk, "What if we have been given different partners?"

"Only one way to find out."

April and Reilly make their way to the desk, looking down at the little cardboard box with finely cut, small rectangular pieces of paper in it. The class is noisy again, with students laughing and complaining about Mr. Arnav's choices. They raise their head to one another, their gaze deep and frigid, April dips her hand into the box and searches for her name. She eventually sees it, and her mouth turns sour, she stares at it for a moment, causing Reilly to be more anxious.

"Well, what is it? Who did you get paired with? Tell me, April," Reilly asks, her voice and body boiling with impatience.

Yet, April couldn't say a word, her mouth was too heavy for that, and she wished she could do something about it. She sees Reilly take the paper from her hand, running her eyes through it.

"Oh my world, you and Nigel!"

CHAPTER FIVE

"Hey, April! Wait up!" Nigel yells out, walking as fast as he could to meet up with her.

It is after school hours, and students are on their way home. Many of which do not have any thought of starting their projects soon, their minds are on other stuff, and wanting to get a project done by the end of the month wasn't exactly at the top of their list.

For April, being paired up with Nigel came as a shocker, one she wasn't expecting. She wanted Reilly, her guts wanted Reilly, her spirit was literally communicating to Mr. Arnav that Reilly would be a better match for her as a partner. Not Nigel. But, here she is now, after the much disappointment she had taken to the face, paired up with the last person she needs right now.

"April, wait," Nigel tells her, stopping her in her steps with a touch on her shoulder, gasping for air, "Woah, you move fast." he says with exhilaration in his eyes.

April sighs, stopping momentarily before continuing her walk forward. Nigel, with his back hunkered and his hands on his knees, still gasping for breath, watches April as she leaves. He furrows his brows in bewilderment, thinking to himself how insensitive she must be right now.

"Are you really going to keep walking? Leaving me here without hearing what I have to say?" He asks her, standing to a spot.

April rolls her eyes, her hands clutched to the strap of her bag, she replies, "You are in the football team, I am sure this is nothing for you."

Feeling defeated and frustrated, mainly due to April's cold treatment, he starts walking toward her. His steps aren't fast or slow, yet he catches up to her in a matter of seconds.

"That's still not enough reason to leave me behind, knowing fully well I want to speak with you," he tells her with an exasperated mien, a bile taste building up in his mouth.

"Alright, I'm sorry. Happy?"

Nigel brushes his hand over his mouth, suppressing in him untold words he would wish to tell April. He feels April isn't treating him right, or taking his feelings into consideration. This is not what he often experiences from other girls, as his charm is enough to get whichever girls he wants. A guy like him, tall and perfectly built, is surely a fantasy for most girls in his school, and they would do almost anything to have him by their side.

But, April is different, she is unlike other girls, doesn't think like them, doesn't act like them. A personality with a shade so different, he feels enthralled by her. April isn't the most beautiful of the girls in school, and Nigel knows, but her person isn't one he could ignore, and so, he tolerated her excesses. No matter how abrasive it may be.

"Anyways, I saw, back in class, that we are–"

"Paired together, I know."

"And, we are to work on the project, and get it finished in three weeks. I know this wasn't the arrangement you were expecting."

"Yet, it happened. What can we do, hmm?"

"Yeah, but I promise, I will be a good partner. I will do anything you ask me to do, name it and it is done. Anything."

April stops to look at him, "It is alright, Nigel. I have heard you, when we begin the research for the project, we shall do it together. So please, stop sounding scared."

Nigel lets out a nervous smile as he rubs his hand at the back of his neck, "Yeah, I…I only want to prove to you I am more than just muscles and charisma. I can be more, April, I can be more to you."

April looks at him with unblinking eyes, searching her head for the best reply she can give. Seconds later, she tells him, "That's very nice of you, Nigel. But, don't forget, this is a class project, so, do well to behave accordingly, okay?"

Nigel doesn't say anything, he only smiles at her with a slightly bruised look and a nod for a reply. April smiles faintly at him before continuing her walk again. She has got some things to do, and felt standing with Nigel was eating deep into her time.

"So, we will see tomorrow?" Nigel asks her, hauling his voice across the concrete sidewalk he is standing on.

April hits against the air with her hand, raising it high, "Yeah, sure, we will."

Moments later, she gets to a bus-stop, on her way to the grocery store to pick up some items for her mother. They will be having a guest later today, and April isn't particularly thrilled about it.

Some minutes later, she arrives at the grocery store, and on her way, she takes out her phone to look through the list of items she needs to get.

'Okay, now, all I need to get is some lettuce, a crate of egg, milk, carrots, eggplants, some broccoli, two rolls of tissue paper, and mineral water. Wonder what she would be doing with mineral water?' she asks herself as she makes it through the electronic door.

She peers at the place for a moment, the bright florescent lights above blasting into her eyes and the gentle touch of the air-conditioning breezing through her skin. And with a plain expression, her phone fixed to the level of her gaze, she starts to walk from aisle to aisle, looking for her items as diligent and as focused as she can be.

She hasn't always been the one to focus, or to remember too. Hence, the need to write down what she needed on her phone. Those two things weren't her forte. She had tried to work on it, like the one time her mother had asked her to go get some stuff at the grocery store, and when April got there, she forgot it all. Or, the time she was sent to get Damien's birthday items from a shop, and she forgot them all again. And, in all those times, she walked back home weary and angry at herself, cursing under her breath as she walked.

This time, she isn't ready to repeat it again.

As minutes clocks into another, April treads aisle after aisle, with her basket in hand and a tired mind, taking off the shelves what she came for. Until the crate of eggs is the only thing remaining.

She takes herself to the aisle the eggs are, ignoring, on her way, the mistreatment a nerd was getting from a group of boys from Daxonhill. She felt like intervening, cutting into their midst and bringing an end to the bullying, but she wasn't ready for that either, she didn't have the energy for it. The nerd was a boy with lean build, thick, brown hair, noodly limbs and a weak and passive mannerism to him. The boys mistreating him found pleasure in knocking off his glasses, and knocking it off again anytime he went to pick it up. April didn't bother herself with it, she shook her head and walked on.

'He will be fine, I believe,' she says as she walks past the scene. She gets to the aisle the eggs are, and goes for the one on her right. She picks it up, and begins walking out of there to where the counter is. Suddenly, she freezes in her steps, a cold air coursing down her spine, then to the rest of her body. She feels her breathing rising and her heart hammering away in her chest, she tries to walk but can't find the strength to do so. She then tries to turn and walk toward where she came from, but a voice in her advises her against it. She curses under her breath, hating this day and what it has made her suffer.

'Why now? Why here? Why does it have to be here?' she asks herself, her chest constricting and heavy.

A moment later, she decides within herself to walk past the figure she is seeing ahead of him, besides, he is looking at the eggs as if studying them. So, he won't be able to spot her with her face inside a blue hood. She inhales and starts walking toward him, steady and slow, almost as though she's walking on glass.

She gets close to him, about to walk past and April feels a moment of relief easing into her. She starts to smile in her hoodie, with her eyes gleaming under the dim cover. She makes to walk into a corner when her heart drops like a sinking anker in a deep sea. The sound of her name being called tied a string-like thread around her heart, causing her little, sharp pains that spread throughout her body.

"April? isn't it?" a male figure asks as he walks toward her, beaming a smile at her.

April turns slowly to face the person behind her, a wry smile on her face which she had to force out, and a stiff, pulsating stance she was trying to loosen. A fuzzy feeling swooped through her body as her eyes caught the deep blue of his eyes, causing her to freeze for a moment.

'Oh my…' she says with a loss of breath.

"Ahh, Kelly? Am I right?" she asks, sounding jovial with her tone.

Kelly shoots a neat smile at her, his hands hidden in his hoodie pockets, "That is right, it's Kelly."

"Hmm, how pleasant to see you, how are you doing? I didn't know you often come here."

Kelly looks around him, as though searching the store, "Uhhmm, yes, I do come here often. You know, I kind of like Daxonhill a little bit. That should be a secret between us by the way."

April looks at him with a curious gaze, which she jettisons with a thought, "That's alright, I can keep secrets, so don't worry."

"I don't think I need to."

Kelly's eyes on her makes April feel drawn to his being, like she's becoming a part of him, something she can touch and hold within her grasp, to feel without any restrictions. Something about him exudes a kind of temperance she has never felt before, and somehow, she feels comfortable around him. And as she stands there, staring at him, and he at her, she remembers she has home to get to.

"Errm, are you done with what you are doing here? I will like to go now." April tells him.

"Oh, yes, I'm done. I only came to get eggs," Kelly swings the egg crate in the air before her.

April then gestures that they should go, and Kelly urges her to move first. And, with a feeling of apprehension, April starts to walk before him, her mind constantly in a battle of what is and what is not. She passes the aisle where the nerd was being bullied, and she sees they are not there anymore. She wonders what could have happened to the nerd. Silently, she wishes security would have come and separated them. But, would they have done so? A question she asks herself.

She and Kelly gets to the counter, and luckily, they are one of the first people to get there. They drop their items, with Kelly offering to pay for April's items. She refuses, but he persists. April allows him, and thought it to be kind gestures. She looks at the cashier, and finds that he is looking at her with a mean look, and somehow, April knew exactly what it meant.

She ignores the man nonetheless till she is done checking out. She takes her stuff which has been arranged inside two polythene bags, and she walks out of the store with Kelly.

"Woah, that man didn't seem to be happy. I wonder what his problem will be?" Kelly asks, smiling to himself.

"Yeah, probably because I am with you, I don't know."

He glances at April with a curious look, searching her face with questioning eyes, "I guess so, which makes me wonder again."

April turns to him with her eyebrows furrowed, and her gaze on him, waiting to hear the next words that would come out of him.

"Why aren't you like them?" he asks her, taking her by surprise with the question.

April searches her mind for a moment, wanting to find an answer to the question. This makes her recount her life and her time in Daxonhill, all she had ever done and still doing, and how she responds to the things around her. She finds out that her way of responding to events happening in Daxonhill, like the issue of bullying or guilt-tripping nerds, is a lot different from the other folks in Daxonhill.

She never liked or wanted to conform with such a life, and has always felt like there is something missing in her that she can't find yet. Regardless, she thinks it ridiculous to hate someone just because they are smarter than you, isn't being smart good? She would ask herself sometimes.

April shrugs, coming to a halt as she reaches her bus-stop, "I don't know, I guess some people are more open with their hate than others."

Kelly nods his head thoughtfully at April's words, "So, you still hate us then?"

April hops into a bus that has just stopped, she replies, "I didn't say that, do I look like I hate you?"

Kelly smiles faintly as he watches April leave with the bus, holding on to her gaze till she takes it away. He looks down to the ground, thinking to himself how peculiar a girl like April is, so welcoming, yet, her personality isn't one to easily figure out. He starts to walk back toward the store when his shoulder brushes against another's.

"Oh, I'm so sorry." Kelly apologizes deeply to the gruff looking man.

"Watch where you're going, you stupid nerd." The man replies, continuing his walk.
Kelly sighs.

***

April gets home a few minutes later, and walks through the door, and when sees there is no one in the living room to exchange greetings with, she goes straight to the kitchen. She starts to put in place all she has gotten from the store, when she feels someone standing behind her, but doesn't actually turn to see who it is. She has two in mind, two guesses, so she doesn't bother to have a look.

"You are back?" the near brittle tone asks.

"Yes, I am," she replies, looking over her shoulder and back at what she was doing, "How was school?" she asks him.

April knew he will be the one, Damien, standing behind her like the ghost he is trying to be. On several occasions would Damien come into a room, and stand like a stiff tree on a spot, watching her till he finally says something. He has done so many times, April has grown used to it. He hears him walking toward a chair near a kitchen counter.

"School was fine, I guess. Always boring in a way, but fine nonetheless."

April sighs, stuffing the milk and eggs into the fridge, "School is always like that, boring and uninteresting."

"Yeah," he says with a tone writhe with questions. He looks up toward April, "Do you know who's coming over today?"

April pauses, looking over her shoulder again, toward where Damien sits, "Should I? Mom didn't mention it."
"It's aunt Maribelle." Damien tells her, coming to an abrupt halt, "She's the one coming over, I heard mom

speaking to her on the phone this afternoon. I just thought of telling you."

"And, I guess I should thank you for ruining my day, right?" she asks sarcastically.

Damien stays quiet, watching as April takes a cup to draw water from the kitchen tap. He thinks about his decision to tell April about aunt Maribelle, and had thought she deserved to know before April does anything uncalled for. Aunt Maribelle is a relative, one April doesn't always agree with, or like for that matter.

"I know you will be able to pass through this one," he tells her, "Just like the former times you stayed with mom and aunt Maribelle, I am certain you can survive this, too."

April gulps her water with a constriction in her throat, she exhales deeply as she finishes, looking toward Damien who has his eyes on her, "And, where will you be during her visit here?"

Damien gets to his feet, walking toward the entrance of the kitchen, "My Jeoffrey's place. Goodbye."

April rolls her eyes, resting her weight against the kitchen counter. She thinks for a moment, imagining what could play out during aunt Maribelle's visit. They are really the best of friends, often disagreeing on various issues, especially when it concerns the nerds. Aunt Maribelle hates the nerds, and often speaks very ill of them. This, inspite of her mother's warnings, makes April correct aunt Maribelle in the most uncouth manner, though her aunt's speech is sometimes to blame.

'It is just for a few hours, and she will be gone, there's no need to worry. My world, why does mom always want me around anyway?' she thinks to herself.

At 6:30 PM, they are in the living room. April's mom, Dareen is seated on a couch wearing a maroon, lace gown. Her face is flushed with cheerfulness and glee as she beams a smile at everything aunt Maribelle says. April is in a corner, on a couch as well with her head burrowed in her phone. She tries as much as she can to zone out of the room, so she wouldn't be able to hear what they are discussing.

"How is it that you are able to work with the nerds when, you know, you don't like them?" Dareen asks her, "I…don't understand." She adds.

Aunt Maribelle muffles a laugh, taking up to her lips vegetables and eggs that had been prepared for her. She is wearing a green, skintight gown with a cape clipped round her shoulders, a slender frame to go with the gown and toned body that exudes excellence in body care. She has deep, piercing brown eyes, one that looks more cynical than charming.

She takes a cup of water after she had swallowed, she gasps, "I am sorry for the late reply—"

Dareen waves her hands at her, "No-no, take your time, there's no rush to it."

Maribelle gives her swift glance, propping herself to speak, "Thank you, Dareen, you are always a kind one. But to answer your question, I would like to understand that there are different ways emotions can be channeled and used. And this goes a long way to determine how great a person you will become, for you are only who you are because of how you decide to use your emotions."

Dareen wears a thoughtful look, her eyes flowing with questions like a running stream. She turns to Maribelle again, "So, what you are saying is that, you are using your hate to get close to the nerds? Is that it?"

"Not quite, my dear Dareen. What I am saying is, I am simply channeling my emotions in a way that enables me to get what I want from them. I still see them as the pretentious rats that they are, but they are rich pretentious rats, and I want a little bit of that riches, do you understand me, Dareen?"

"So, you are pretending as well?" Dareen asks with an arched brow, almost convinced about Maribelle's motives.

Maribelle gasps suddenly, spewing little bits of the water in her mouth, "I am not pretending, Dareen, why would you think that?"

Dareen feels apprehended by her sister's sudden outburst, "I'm sorry, I thought that was what you meant."

"No-no, what I meant is, I am only giving them a taste of their own medicine, I am not pretending."

"Sounds like you are pretending to me," says April, her head still burrowed in her phone.

Dareen and Maribelle turn their gaze toward April, with Maribelle's eyes flaring up with subtle agitation. She suppresses it the best she could, heaving her body as calmly as she can till she is calm enough to reply. She feels her mind seething with thoughts, and thinks how poorly she must have been misunderstood. She tries to calm herself regardless.

"April? Didn't you hear what she said?" Dareen asks in a bid to further calm the rising tension in the room.

"Leave her, Dareen. She is still young, she will grow and understand how our society works." Maribelle takes a jab at her.

This further increases the air of tension swirling in the room. April raises her gaze to Maribelle's cynical eyes, looking into them with a face fraught with disinterest.

"Or, maybe understand that some people do not deserve where they are in life. So, instead of me trying to get the acknowledgement of others for something I'm not, I think I will just sit put in my house and binge watch movies to my taste."

Maribelle bites her lips in a sneer, staring at April with furious eyes that grow even more furious as April doesn't seem to be scared by her. She hates it anytime an argument breaks out between them, it irks her, making her stomach turn and turn, twisting itself inside of her. She hates that it hurts her head, and makes her breathing shallow and hot. But, in all their arguments about the nerds, she has never felt as pained as now.

She exhales deeply, "Child, if you know what I have done to get to where I am presently, you will know that it takes much more than being a pretentious sycophant to get here. And just so you know, the nerds all have needs and wants, they only follow you for what you can offer them, if you don't have that, you are nothing but a bag full of air. You will know this when you finally encounter one."

She stares at her aunt for a while, thinking about her words. April tries to convince herself that she is wrong and too generic with her statement, not all nerds are selfish as she has stated, and not all as she claims. "Whatever, I am out of here," she gets up, walking toward the stairs, "And, I am not a child."

Maribelle laughs silently, a feeling that she has won yet again twirling all around her, "You are if you still think there is an exception in the mannerisms of the nerds, because there is not."

April stops, narrowing her gaze at her aunt. She says in a near whisper, "You don't know what you are saying."

"The 5 years I have spent in Anthera tells me I do. Trust me, when you are older, you will get to know what I know. But, for the meantime, stay away from them, they will break you beyond recognition."

"Says the woman who's trying to be like the nerds, but can't, only pretending her way up to their noses." She says harshly, trotting up to her room.

"April?" her mother calls out in caution.

"Let her be, sister" Maribelle tells her, placing a hand over her sister's hand, "I am not angry, I only hope she comes to realize how true I am. I only hope."

The next sound they hear comes from a door been banged against its frame. April's door.

CHAPTER SIX

It is another morning, another school day, but unlike the other days April would get up feeling too exhausted already about school, she woke up with the thought of yesterday on her mind. She tries to wave it away, but it seems her mind isn't complying with her demands. She hates it when she can't let go of a thought, as she would always find herself recalling the images again and again, to the point of exhaustion. She sighs as she drags herself out of bed.

An hour and a half later, she trudges to the dining room where everyone else is already seated and eating. Their gaze soon reverts to April who just entered the room, bringing with it a silence so loud, it echoes.

She walks to the dining table, her face expressionless and almost drooping, her eyes deep with hidden emotions, she takes her seat and sets herself to start eating. Glances are exchanged between Morris, Dareen, and Damien, with Damien looking more puzzled than his parents. He darts his curious eyes from April to his mother and back to April, hoping someone would notice and give him an answer. But, such an answer never came.

"Good morning, April, how was your night?" her mother asks, wearing a quaky smile and a concerned look.

April shrugs her shoulders, "It was fine… I guess. I'm sorry, good morning, mom…dad."

"Good morning, April." Her father responds, nodding his head with it.

Dareen smiles, her eyes often rising toward April as she eats. April still maintains her brooding look, eating her food without a word to anybody, and this unsettles them all, especially Damien, though he has a guess what might have caused her murky mood this morning.

Damien eats his food with his eyes constantly staring at April, searching her face and their mother's. He sees the mother is a bit concerned, the edges of her lips drooping downward, her gaze often shifting to April, full of worry and anticipation. Almost as if something terrible happened, or did happen. He adjusts himself on his chair, wanting to say something.

"So, mom, how was aunt Maribelle's visit yesterday?" Damien asks, maintaining a firm eye on his mother as he waits for her answer.

She hesitates to reply, swallowing and looking toward April's melancholic expression. She turns to Damien, "Yeah, aunt Maribelle's visit yesterday was fine, it is not like anything out of usual happened. Just the normal stuff."

"Hmm," Damien nods his head with a convincing tint to his face, "That's nice, I guess. Just that, anytime April's like this after aunt Maribelle's visits, it is usually because–"

"Enough, Damien," his father tells him, his voice stiff and firm. This stops Damien from talking any further, "Eat your food, you have school to go to." He adds.

Damien says nothing as takes another look at April's colorless face, sensing she must have gotten into another argument with their aunt last night. He wishes he was there, when they were arguing, that way he would know what they argued about. Now, all he can do is guess, and guesses often doesn't help it.

A few minutes later, everyone's done with their breakfast, and April is now in the kitchen, standing beside the sink with a glass cup in hand as she fills it with water. She sees her mother walk up close to her, dropping some dirty plates into the sink.

She says nothing to the mom, taking the glass cup up to her mouth. She hears her mother sigh, knowing she is about to speak.

"Maribelle can be difficult at times, a little unreasonable if you ask me," her mother starts to speak to her, "But, that's who she is, I don't want you to get angry at that fact."

April lets out a contented sigh after she has finished drinking her water. She says to the mom, "Even when she's saying something wrong?"

Dareen shrugs with doubt all over her face, "Well, she sometimes makes a point."

April groans with exhaustion, walking away from the sink counter, "She is not making any point, mom. All I see is a woman who's not comfortable in her own skin, and while I don't see anything wrong in seeking improvement or riches, as she said, she shouldn't be lying about it. And, you know she doesn't really hate the nerds, she's only saying that to cover her weakness."

"April, don't say that, we are not sure of that."

April backpedals out of the kitchen, "Well, I am, mom. And, I am sure she shivers anytime she's with the nerds, trying very hard to impress. Even her way of speaking gave her out."

Dareen rolls her eyes in defiance to April's words, she raises her voice across the kitchen so April would hear, "However it may be, April, always take it easy with your aunt, you hear me."

April doesn't reply. She walks out of the house and into the open air to meet Reilly already waiting for her. Her eyes widened into a circle as she wasn't expecting Reilly to be out so soon. Then it hit her. She is the one that is late, and Reilly has been waiting for her.

"What took you so long? I have been standing here for hours." Reilly laments hysterically, almost playful in her tone.

"I am so sorry, Reilly, it was my mom. She was…you know what? Just forget it."

Reilly arches her brow in confusion, hit by the fact that April doesn't want to share something with her. She waves it off, and decides not to speak about it.

"Okay, but please, be quick next time."

"Why didn't you just go sit by the front porch? That

could have been better."

Reilly lowers her lips as she realizes her folly, she attempts to cover it up, "I didn't know you would take that long, I would have gone to sit, but then, I thought you would come out any second."

April turns a sly, side glance at Reilly, the edge of her lips raised in a mocking smile, "And when I didn't come out seconds later?"

Reilly stops walking, waving her hands in the air as though waving the talk away, "You know what, April, let's forget that I stood by your lawn this morning, waiting for you. You hear me, let's forget it."

April kept walking, and with a playful grin on her face, she replies Reilly while backpedaling, "Alright, if you say so."

And then, she stops, so Reilly could walk up to her. But, before Reilly could get to her, her phone starts to ring out. Reilly gets curious.

"Who is calling?"

April rolls her eyes, digging into her back pocket for her phone, "Probably, Nigel."

Reilly smiles, which makes April look at her oddly and with a teasing stare. Reilly doesn't respond to it, but gestures to her to check her phone. April checks it, and the glee that was once on her face morphs quickly into one of confusion. The number calling isn't one of Nigel's, but of another's.

She takes the call, "Hello?"

"Hello, April, it's me, Kelly." Says Kelly on the other end.

April's body went cold when she held it as Kelly spoke, she tilts her head toward Reilly, who meets her with a curious arch to her brows.

"Hey, you…how are you doing?" April asks him with a friendly tone, so as not to raise suspicion in Reilly.

"Oh, I am well, Reilly. I am pretty sure you are on your way to school right this moment, am I right?"

She hesitates for a moment, almost not listening anymore, "Uhh, yeah-yeah, that's right. Just as you said, I am on my way to school. Ha-ha, that's right."

She looks at Reilly again, her eyes are not on her, but April hopes she isn't able to hear who she is speaking with.

"Uhh, yes, I forgot to tell you how I got your number."

"Trust me, I would like to know more than anything in this world."

"Woah, you sound furious."

"Well?"

April turns to look at Reilly again, and their eyes meet. She takes her gaze away as she feels uncertain about how to explain herself when she's done talking.

"Right. Onto how I got your number. I got it from one

of your social media pages, it was just there for the taking, and I thought, since we know each other now, maybe you wouldn't mind getting a call from me. You don't, right?"

April exhales silently, her eyes on the road. She thinks for a while before responding, "It's alright, I think. But, I have got to go now."

"That's right, you have school to get to. I believe we shall be talking again."

"Maybe, and bye for now."

She ends the call, her hands shaking from the thought of speaking with a nerd who just called her out of the blue. It all doesn't make sense to her, and she wonders why Kelly would be going through her social media page.

As April walks to the bus-stop, with Reilly walking beside her, she clenches her hands out of nervousness, her mind hurting her with the thought of Kelly being a recurring figure in her life. A figure she is not intending to keep around.

"So, are we both going to pretend you didn't just finish speaking with that nerd, or am I talking too much?" Reilly says to her with a sarcastic undertone.

April's fears manifests as it stands, staring her in the eyes.

'She heard it?' April asks herself.

April shrugs it off, trying to look unfazed, "I didn't know he was going to call, besides, it is not a big deal."

Reilly scoffs, a maniacal smile tearing through her face,

"You do not learn, do you? And from the looks of it, you don't even want to."

April pauses in her walk, peering at Reilly with perplexed eyes. Reilly doesn't stop, her hands wrapped to the straps of her bag and her head propped up, she doesn't bother to look April's way even when she has stopped moving.

"Reilly? It is not like that." April says, raising her voice and picking up her pace again. But, Reilly didn't give her a response, not even a sound was made.

***

As they got to school and went through their classes, April and Reilly didn't speak of what happened earlier. April didn't try to convince Reilly, neither did Reilly say anything to her about it. It was as though they had all put the event behind them, not to talk about it or let it rear its ugly head in their friendship.

But, it didn't go without April thinking every few seconds why Reilly hasn't made as much as a fuss about it, to caution her about her association with Kelly, or lecture her on how terrible the nerds can be. Reilly hadn't done any of those, and it pricked April in the pores of her skin.

Throughout most of time together in school, her ears waited to hear what would come after Reilly's laugh, the inference she would make after commenting on the nerds and a feat they had accomplished, she looked on to see if Reilly would say anything regarding her unexpected phone call with Kelly. She observed, she watched, she waited. Yet, nothing came, and an atmosphere of relief formed inside as she continued her normal flow and chat with her best friend. Reilly.

'And, what exactly will I give this project?' April asks herself.

She is inside the school's library, sitting on a chair with her arms folded on a brown, wooden table. There are other students inside with her as well, but there are only a handful in the near noiseless, large room. She peers at something, her eyes thoughtful and distant, and equally bleeding with unanswered questions.

She is currently searching through the flicks of roaming thoughts in her head as she tries to find the right topic for their topic. Nigel was supposed to be with her, to help her share ideas, so they can get their project on the way. And now, he isn't with her to do that, she is finding it a little difficult thinking anything up.

'Would he be able to even suggest a name for the project? Brains hasn't been one of Nigel's best strengths.' She tells herself.

She has been with Nigel longer than she can remember, and know how much he has changed and grown. And, being someone she has known for as long as Reilly – over 10 years – Nigel hadn't given himself the thought to give his academics or school much effort. He rather splurges his time on football practices and training, getting fit, and entertaining every girl in school – though this has waned in the last few days.

April groans, rubbing her hands painfully across her face in self-defeat, she lets her head fall to her folded hands. She lets out a long sigh.

'What am I going to do now? Call Kelly? … No way! I don't need any nerd helping me. Though, that wouldn't be a bad idea.' She is thinking of a solution.

April jerks her head up swiftly, her eyes open and resolute. She decides within herself a topic will be created and research started on it immediately. There is still a lot of time till the submission date, but if she's going to get a good score, she needs to work with dexterity of mind. Like a nerd would, she thinks to herself, a half smile creaking through her face.

She exhales deeply, taking in deep breaths as though preparing for an arduous task, she takes the book beside her and starts flipping through the pages. Certainly, something in it will interest her, and might bring about the topic she so much desires.

'We have been told to do research about the prehistoric times and its animals, and since it is something I enjoy so much, this shouldn't be a problem for me then. Choosing what to write on shouldn't be a problem.'

But, it is a problem. April hasn't yet realized how long it can take her to figure something out, it takes her longer time to think, to calculate, and put the different pieces together. She always struggles with this aspect of her life, though when determined, April can surprise herself as well.

'Okay, write on whatever topic you so choose, Mr. Arnav said, and I choose…' April says as her mind considers the various possible options in front of her.

Her face soon lights with an explosion of excitement

and a sense of accomplishment as she finally stumbles on a topic she considers fit to research on. She jumps up in excitement, letting out a loud "Yes!" when the idea finally comes to her, swimming in the euphoria of her own self-lit sensation.

Her joy and laughter persists for a moment, that she starts to get annoyed looks from the others in the library. April soon notices the furrowed stares, a feeling of shame and guilt filling her up inside, she goes to her seat and sits down very quietly. Yet, the smile on her face doesn't fade as it remains like dry paint on a building.

'And that … And, that is what we are going to do." She tells herself in the moment.

"Hey? Sorry for being so late," says Nigel, taking a seat beside her, all smiles and oozing with charm.

April stays silent for a moment, trying to quell the flowing gladness in her heart. She turns to Nigel with a friendly smile, "Where have you been? Anyway, that doesn't matter, I have got our research topic, and I would like us to begin work immediately."

"Already? The last time we spoke, you said you haven't–"

"Well, I do now, Nigel, is there a problem?" she asks stiffly, peering into Nigel's eyes with an unflinching gaze.

Nigel feels a bit intimidated, but still maintains his composure, "Ahh, no, there's no problem at all."

April tilts her backwards, her lips curled a little smuggishly. She says cheerfully, "Alright, let's do this thing."

April takes a book to her face, about to get it open when she hears Nigel's voice flow across her shoulder to her ears. She didn't hear him correctly, her mind couldn't let her, she was still stuck in her happiest moment.

"Huh? What did you say?" she asks him, her gaze on him again.

He smiles, shifting his chair, so he can face her properly, "I ask, what topic did you come up with? What are we working on?"

April stifles a laughter, an explosion happening in her again. She replies, "I forgot to tell you–"

"It's alright, I can always wait for pretty girls to take their time." He tells her, cutting her short.

She narrows her eyes at him, finding his statement a bit odd, "Okay…anyway, what we will be doing will be on prehistoric animals, yes, but we will focus on their periods of their existence, what they fed on, and what they fed on them in the case of prey and predator. You understand, right?"

"Yeah," Nigel replies, beaming his perfect set of teeth at April, searching her eyes as she looks into his, "I think it's a very cool topic if you ask me. Way better than others."

"Really?" April asks curiously, her eyes wide for an answer.

Nigel reclines into his seat, "Absolutely, it is almost as though you are a nerd yourself, and I don't even like them. I guess when those smarts are coming from a Daxonhill girl such as you, it makes all the difference."

April's face is flushed with pink as Nigel's words lifts her from her seat. She feels happy that someone acknowledges her for the effort she has made, for thinking, and making sure something has been done toward a problem. She doesn't always get these kinds of words, and hearing it now makes her feel like a winner ready to conquer.

"Thank you, Nigel," she tells him, "I really appreciate it." April adds, taking up the textbook to her face again.

Nigel watches her for a moment, his fingers tapping on the table as he contemplates his thoughts. She adjusts on the chair, sitting upright, and running a prying eye round the library, before fixing it back on April again. He sighs, shifting the chair in its former position, his arms on the table, still tapping away on it. He turns to April again and then to the book in front of her, he bites his lips, and makes to speak.

"I was thinking, April," he says finally, a nervous stream of cold rushing through his body, "If I can…I mean, if we can hang out sometime? I promise, I won't bring any talk about the nerds."

The brightness to April's mood dims, an unsettling feeling creaking through her body as she tries to find a reply to Nigel's question. An outing isn't something she is intending to do anytime soon, April hardly goes out anyway to consider a date with Nigel. And besides, she isn't thinking about having anything to do with a guy at the moment. At least, not now.

"Well? What do you say?" Nigel asks, peering curiously into April's still eyes.

She maintains a stiff composure, looking back into her book, "You do know we have a project at hand, right?"

"We can sometimes talk about it over some smoothies."

"While taking a stroll in a park."

"Yes!"

"No!" she tells him, raising her head to him. She closes her eyes, letting out a restive breath, her body heaving as she gives herself a moment to think, "Nigel, what we have now is a little bit too important to consider your request. Maybe, when all this is done, I can think about it, what do you think?" April adds, hoping that it appeals to Nigel's hopes. Though, she doesn't see herself ever going out with him.

"I think you are just trying to shut me up, April."

"And, why would I do that? I am only telling you what I think, if you are not okay with you, then fine. We leave it at that." She tells him, shifting her gaze to her book again.

Nigel searches her face with doubtful eyes, shaking his head and rolling his rolls when he couldn't come up with a proper counter to April's words. He props himself with a groan, looking into the far distance of the library.

"Alright, April. Whatever you say, after our project, we get to hang out."

"I will consider it." she tells him, giving him a side look. Words she might never apply.

CHAPTER SEVEN

It has been a long school hour, treacherous, daunting, and downright annoying for every student at Daxonhill High, which is why when the bell goes off for dismissal, spirits are lifted and sighs of relief are breathed out. A respite from their tormenting stay in class, something they all thought long and overdue.

It is another hour for dismissal, students are scattered everywhere around the school premises and also inside the buildings. But, not for long, they would come out sooner or later.

April comes out of the school building and into the open surrounding of its premises. She tilts her head from the right to the left, peering through the many heads of students going about their various activities. She is looking for Reilly, to walk home with her. That is, if Reilly is still her friend anyway.

Minutes into her search, she sees a girl with purple hair, dark hose and a black, skintight skirt that fits nicely to her curves and bum. A bum April sometimes envies due to its round figure. She recognizes it's Reilly, her purple hair was unmistakable. She takes a deep breath, looking through her thoughts for the best thing to say, the words that would not further make her agitated.

She sees Reilly is done with speaking with a couple of students, her project partner is there with her, Daisy's her name and she is the one Reilly is speaking to at the moment. April begins to walk toward them, slow and trepid in her movement, she prepares herself for the worst.

Before she gets to Reilly, Daisy walks off, waving a hand at Reilly. A perfect moment for whatever will come out from their meeting.

"Reilly, great seeing you here, wanna walk home?" April asks, her eyes squinting under the sun as she expects Reilly to turn her down.

Reilly doesn't answer her right away, she stares at April for a moment, as though thinking of what to say. This makes April a little uncomfortable, anxious, and shaking in the knees. Her friend's silence is as cold as the ice on a winter morning, but if this is what she would go through before getting a reply, then she shall stay this way.

"Okay, let's go." Says Reilly, moving forward ahead of April.

That took her by surprise, Reilly's reply. She had thought Reilly was angry, was supposed to be angry at her, and avoided her on all accounts. But, that isn't the case, and it surprises April to no end, her head constantly looking for an explanation to justify Reilly's nice treatment toward her. It is odd, unusual, a side of Reilly she hasn't seen before, a side of Reilly she will like to continue to see.

"Hey, April," Reilly calls out to her, her hand in the air so April can see her, "Aren't you coming?" she asks her with a raised voice.

April snaps herself out of her thoughts, adjusting the strap of her backpack around her shoulder, and with a somewhat relaxed mind, she starts to run toward Reilly. A few seconds later, she gets to her, almost out of breath, with her words inaudible due to it.

"Why…why aren't you angry at me? For earlier?" she asks her, trying to ease her flooded lungs.

"I am not angry at you. I mean, I was, but I saw it as added stress to my health, so I left it. I still want to live, you know?" Reilly says jokingly, almost letting out a laugh.

"Oh, I hadn't thought of it that way. You know, most times–"

"I am against the nerds talking to you or wanting to get close, especially that Kelly of a guy, I know. And, trust me, I still hate them, but I will be…what's the word, sparing with my comments, especially when it comes to you," Reilly tells her with a smile on her face.

April tries to speak, but gets cut short when she sees the scowled brows of Reilly's eyes. She is looking up ahead at something, and when April looks toward her front, she sees it's someone instead. Someone who's coming at the wrong time. Her gaze goes back to Reilly's face, and imagines the war and stifling air that is to follow from this encounter.

"And, just when you are talking about them, that's when they think to pop out their awful heads." Reilly says with a contorted mien.

The afternoon wind pushes up to April's face, but it has little effect on her as her body goes numb and her throat goes dry. Kelly is walking toward them, and the only thing on her mind is, how did he locate her here?

'Is he stalking me?' April asks herself.

Kelly gets close, her white teeth gleaming under the afternoon sun, his pale, smooth skin glowing and tanned enough to pass for a fashion model. He stops before with an air of confidence that doesn't seem to waver under the spiteful gaze of Reilly. He doesn't seem to care about that, and at that moment, April suddenly envies him for that.

"Good afternoon, ladies," he greets them, a grin on his face and his speech fluid and clear.

"What are you doing here? Don't you have somewhere else to be? Hope you didn't come to look for April?" Reilly asks, walking closer and closer to him the more he walks back.

"Okay," he says, feeling uncomfortable, but still maintaining a smile, "That's a lot of questions. Three, actually, but it's a lot."

"Answer!" Reilly demands harshly.

Kelly's face turns white, staring at Reilly with searching eyes. He begins to stutter, "Errm, yes, in a way, your suspicions are correct."

"I knew it," says Reilly, looking at April's timid face, "I knew you would come here for her, for April. Why?"

Kelly digs his fingers into his hair in a state of nervousness, his eyes to the floor, "It is not what you think, April's friend, I was actually coming from a place here in Daxonhill when I thought it wouldn't be a bad idea to come check out April's school."

"Lies!" Reilly spits out loudly, almost drawing the attention of others.

Kelly, however, didn't escape the stares nerds get whenever they are in Daxonhill, almost as if they can be perceived from miles away. He tries to hide that attribute of himself away, tucked away under the disguise of a basic person, wearing their clothes, smelling like them, and sometimes, acting like them. But, it doesn't seem to work, his smarts always surfaces, casting a shadow over all his antics.

The urge to run home swirls inside April, rising from her feet to her stomach, and then to her arms. She feels herself drifting away, like the wind giving her the help and push you needed to escape this torturous moment. Yet, she is disappointed that her whole body cannot give in to this urge, and she is left standing there, mute and confused, and wishing this is all a dream.

But, it isn't a dream. It is her reality, a sickening reality that she has to balance and handle properly else, her decisions might come back to haunt her. As she stands there, listening to Reilly and Kelly go at it neck to neck, she thinks of what to do.

"April, let's go." Reilly tells her, her eyes mean and abrasive on Kelly. She starts to move forward.

April doesn't move, and she hates it that she cannot move. Why couldn't she take a step forward like Reilly has? Why are her legs doing this to her? And then, she remembers that there are times one must do something good for one's self, even if it inconveniences others. Her heart burns as she does this, her legs turning into water, still like a calm sea. And yet, she feels her friend might just be overreacting.

'Is it that serious, Reilly? Is it that serious? Kelly is just another person. Let's see him as one, can't we?' April says within herself, wishing those words could be easily said to Reilly.

Reilly swallows, clenching her teeth as she looks at April for a moment, realization setting in that April is complacent, unwilling to go home with her. Her eyes start to burn with a furious storm she tries to suppress. She swallows again, and she feels her throat constricted and hurting, and the taste in mouth has gone sour.

She feels betrayed at this moment, alone under a cold bridge, alone even though her best friend stands a few metres away from her. A moment she will definitely dread a lot.

"So, you are not going to walk with me?" Reilly asks in a near whisper, her body almost shaky where she stands.

April begins to walk toward her, extending her hand to touch Reilly, "It is not like that, Reilly, it's just that–"

"Don't. Don't even…" Reilly comes to a pause, the air around her stiffening the more she breathes in. She tries to finish her words, but couldn't, and she turns to continue walking, leaving April standing alone.

"Reilly?" April calls out to her, but she doesn't turn or respond.

April's body slumps against its weight, a dark cloud looming over her as she broods over Reilly walking away from her. If only Reilly could wait and see what she sees, she wouldn't be in this type of situation, having her friend having a wall of distrust built around her isn't something she considers healthy.

She thinks that Reilly needs a change of perception, but how can that happen when her eyes seem too blind to see, and her lips too quick to conclude. It reels her up sometimes, though she knows she will change her someday.

"I am so sorry for what just happened, I didn't…mean to disrupt whatever you have going on." Kelly tells her over her shoulders.

April sighs, her eyes still on Reilly, "It's okay, she is sometimes like this, she will come around."

April hopes she comes around, just as she hadn't been angry with her earlier today, maybe she won't be angry with her still. Reilly might not speak to her for a while, but after some few days, April knows they will come back again. They are almost inseparable, no matter the hubris that gets blown up as dust over their faces, and she likes that they share such a bond.

She groans as she begins to walk, speaking softly, "Everytime this happens, I always find myself overthinking things. And it hurts my head so much, I hate it."

Kelly walks behind her, "And, do you often talk about it with her?"

"Not really. Sometimes, we apologize, but most times, we

just go on talking with each other again like nothing happened. But before that, we would stay not talking to each other for some days. It's crazy, I know."

Kelly eyes peers thoughtfully at her, a faint smile teasing his lips. He shoves both his hands into his pocket, ignoring the spiteful gazes of people around him, while still maintaining his smile. Though, it discomforts him.

"You know what I think?"

April raises her gaze to him, "No, what is it?"

"The strongest relationships and bonds are built on the foundation of fluid and lucid communication between both parties. If you and your friend go days without talking to each other, it can create a void you would end up trying to fill again. Why wait for it to get to that level when you can just walk up to her, and speak to her about how you feel and how you would want to resolve the matter. Do you understand?"

April nods a reply, their walk taking a slow pace.

"Unless, maybe both of you are proud, which–"

She arches her brows in exasperation, her lips lowering to her jaws as she cuts in quickly, "We are not proud."

"Which…I know you are not," he completes his sentence, "I believe it is just a girl-like thing to do."

April makes to respond to him, but her attention soon gets drawn to some group of guys who are hurling hateful and degrading words at Kelly. There are four of them in a car, and April recognises them to be boys in her school. She knows this is how they behave, so she isn't surprised.

She looks up at Kelly's face to see his reaction and his calmness speaks so loudly of his personality. He only looks at them and smiles, and she feels like asking him where he finds the strength to brush off words that could pierce the heart deep enough to scar. But, she thinks against it, and leaves it to another time.

"I believe this is where we go our separate ways." She says as she gets to the bus-stop, beaming a smile at him.

***

It is dinner time at April's home, everyone is at the dining table, clanking spoons against her plates as they all dig into their meals—mashed potatoes with fish and vegetables. Their faces are as light and as bright as it can be, though Morris' and Dareen's are the brightest. Gleaming as though they have something to spill out.

They have been looking at each other since they started eating, eyes glancing and passing coded signals to one another, hesitating in their speech, and looking at their children while they eat.

April and Damien are obviously unaware of what's going on between their parents, the stares, the little laughter, the tilting of heads toward their direction, and even more stares. All of which are going on unnoticed by them.

However, that is certain to happen, apart from being engrossed in good cooking, April and Damien have their eyes glued to the screens of their phones, scrolling and eating at the same time, which will make it almost impossible for them to notice anything unusual with their parents. April has her earbuds even, therefore she can't hear her parents giggling or whispering, as her attention is no longer in the room.

Morris and Dareen exchange a nod of acquiescence amongst themselves, coming to a stop in their meal and setting themselves to speak. Dareen taps the table gently, which brings their children's attention to them as they all raise their heads to them. April still doesn't take her earbuds off.

"Your father has–" Dareen says, coming to a stop as her eyes fall on April sternly, "April, take off your earbuds." She says stiffly.

April hesitates, and with a begrudged expression on her face, she takes them and drops them into its case on the table. A tired, disinterested look on her face, she awaits when her parents will start talking. "Okay, your father has something cool to tell us all, though I know, but hey, we are family, aren't we?" She tells them with a pleasing smile, turning to Morris and gesturing to him to speak.

Their father gets himself, clearing his throat and adjusting in his chair, "Do you all remember the job I said I was going to apply for? Well, I did and guess what?"

"What?" asks April, though she likely knew the answer.

"I got the job!" Morris explodes with excitement, swinging his hand in the air as Dareen and Damien clap happily for you.

April smiles faintly at her father, she feels proud of him for getting what he wanted. She had thought such a thing cannot be done by him, that the job won't be given to him due to his incapacity for it. April was wrong, she had thought wrong and she stupid for it now. How could her father look at her now, she is sure he would look at her as a cynical person that didn't believe he was up to something as big as being a product manager. She is happy for him nonetheless.

"I am happy for you, dad. Congratulations." She tells him, her tongue sinking into her jaw.

"Yes, thank you, April. Thank you." He tells her, his voice still lofty from a sense of accomplishment.

Minutes later, the dining table turns into one of various talks and laughter about Morris' new job, questioning flying here and there, and Morris answering them as best as he could, though with a newfound confidence.

They soon stop talking as their voices decimate into the air around them, an echoing vacuum filling the very room they are in. They hear the sound again, someone is knocking on the door, their front door, and their eyes exchange quick looks at one another.

"Is anyone expecting anyone tonight?" Dareen asks.

April and Damien shake their heads in a reply. Damien gets out his chair.

"I will go check who it is." He tells them as he leaves for the door.

Moments later, Damien returns to the dining room, his eyes darting from his parents to April, standing in an atmosphere of apprehension around him.

"Well?" April urges him to speak.

"Someone is outside, and he says he would like to see April, says his name's Nigel."

April's brows break in surprise, "What! What's he doing here?" April turns to her parents, and tells them she would be back soon. Damien takes his seat, giving way for April to walk past.

She gets to the door, and sees it's truly Nigel at the door, looking down into her unpleasant face.

"What are you doing here, Nigel? Can't you see it's kind of late?" she snaps at him.

Nigel smiles at her, "It's only 7:45, it isn't that late."

April folds her arms around her chest, looking stiffly into Nigel's calm eyes, "What are you doing here?"

"I came to see you, I didn't know this is what I would get if I come."

"Maybe, you wouldn't get it if you had called at least."

"Well," he says, rubbing a hand over his face nervously, "Since, you are pissed already, I might as well say it out."

"What is it?"

"I…I saw you today with a nerd, and–"

April flares up, "Oh my, Nigel, this is what you came here to tell me? About a nerd you saw me with?"

"I was only worried."

"Well, don't be. You have no reason to be worried, I and the person you saw today shouldn't get you worked up. I am perfectly fine on my own."

She makes to close to the door, but couldn't as Nigel stops it with his hand.

"April, wait," he tells her with a pleading face, "It is not what you think, I am trying to look out for you, to show you that I care."

April stares into his face for a while, hesitating to reply him. She sighs, "Thank you, Nigel, but I have enough people looking out for me already. And, if you would excuse me, I need to go inside now. See you tomorrow."

April closes the door gently, leaving Nigel to his devices. As she closes the door, he feels a stream of shame coursing through his body, a feeling of regret for his action. He runs a hand through his hair with eyes misty from regret, thinking how terrible it has been coming all the way to April's house to tell her he cared for her. A stupid move on his part.

Nigel exhales deeply, feeling cold and weak, and his body pricking with tingling pain. He decides, within himself, he would start doing things a little more differently, for he was tired of hurting April.

CHAPTER EIGHT

On the far south of Daxonhill, there is a city so excellent-ly built, it marvels even the folks at Daxonhill. Whenever they come or pass through their gates, their eyes will be lit with awe and amazement as they stare at the magnificent buildings, infrastructures, trains and cars and even buses. They would be looking at the skyscrapers, the properly constructed roads, and the way the people here have been able to grow plants around their houses. Something they think to be odd and somewhat foolish, yet, with the beauty that it depicts, their mouths still droop at the elegance and greenery of these plants.

This is one of the places one would come, and the place will be nearly noiseless, as no one is saying much to one an-other, only speaking when the need arises. Their cars and buses are near noiseless, moving along the road with only a hum of an engine to be heard. And their style of dressing, neat, spotless, and minimal, suitable for the warm weather, is another notable factor for the people of Anthera. Of-ten carrying out their duties in the most sane manner, and without too much huffing and puffing.

However, their inner city isn't as noiseless as the neigh-borhoods in it, where they are low buildings situated on a very large expanse of land, most of which are behind fenced and gated estates — for privacy purposes. And in one of these neighborhoods is Kelly's home, owned by his millionaire father. Who is almost always not home, except on weekends and whenever there aren't any meetings.

"I am certain today, I am going to score against you, Olan. Just you wait," Kelly says to a man a bit older than him. They are on a tennis court, about to commence their game.

"I am certain too, master Kelly. You have been getting good these past few days, almost beating me in some matches," Olan answers him, steadying himself and taking a position.

Kelly smirks, knitting his brows together, "Don't patronize me, Olan."

Kelly raises the ball high into the air, striking it with great force to the left side of Olan's position. Olan sees it, and with a quick sprint, runs toward the ball, hitting it back at Kelly. Kelly manages to strike back as well, though with flooded lungs. He is certain Olan will not get this hit this time, but he was wrong and the smile on his face vanishes. He runs toward the incoming lime-colored ball, jumping into the air to cover more distance; he hits it back at Olan, though he nearly missed. He heaves his chest exhaustively, his eyes on the ball as he waits for it.

"Kelly, mother sends for you," says a girl who has just entered through a door. Small, slender, with hair packed into a ponytail, and wearing a white gown that's a little below her knees. She has her eyes on Kelly and the game he is playing, tight-lipped in the face and getting impatient standing there. "Kelly, I said mother is looking for you."

Kelly frantically runs toward the ball to hit it back, "Can you not see I am trying to win here? Go, I will be on my way soon."

She exhales a hot breath, "I wish I could walk through that door right now, and go tell mother that–"

"Good." Kelly tells her from across the court.

"But, unfortunately, I can't. As you can see, mother has made it clear to me not to come back without you, ss though I am responsible for you. I mean, what is that?" she laments, obviously seething where she stands.

"And what did father say about it?" he asks, striking a ball back at Olan, panting and sweating profusely.

"What would he say? He has nothing to say," she tells him, raising her voice a bit higher, "Besides, he doesn't look too happy today." She says with a low tone.

"What did you say?" Kelly asks, coming to a pause as he stares at her with a vacant face.

The girl looks up at him, straightening her face again, "I said come to lunch with me or mother will not be pleased. This is my final word on this."

Kelly stays looking at the girl with a thoughtful look, so much that he hears the faint sound of a ball being hit and approaching him. He turns toward the ball's direction, and in a heartbeat, begins running at it to strike it back. Sadly, he wasn't fast enough as the ball crossed beyond his reach.

He sighs, raising his gaze at the girl, "Look what you

made me do now, Tiana."

Tiana's lips form a smirk, "Such defeat was inevitable anyway, I have watched you fail more times than I could count. So, what does it matter?"

Kelly walks up to her, flipping the racket in his hand and grinning, "It matters, you know why? Today was the day I finally beat Olan, and I was on the verge, until you came along."

"Really?" Tiana asks disinterestedly.

She turns her gaze to the left, toward Olan, who has been watching them at the far left side of the tennis court, commanding him to come over. Which he does by dispersing into pixel-like mist, and then, reappearing in the midst of Tiana and Kelly.

"Here I am, master Tians. Is anything the problem?" Olan asks with a slightly honeyed tone.

With a fixed gaze on Kelly, she asks Olan, "How many times has Kelly won tennis matches against you?"

"0 times, master Tiana." Olan replies, offsetting Kelly in a way as he twirls himself in a circle, though still with a smile.

"And, how many times have you won against him, Olan?" she asks with a smuggish look on her face, her eyes narrowed and brows arched.

"46 times, master Tiana. And counting today's defeat, that would make it–"

"47 times."

"That's correct, master Tiana."

"So, you see, your defeat was inevitable," she tells him, turning around and walking toward the entrance, "Hurry, mother is waiting." Tiana adds.

Kelly looks at Olan with a lowered, wanting to know he wasn't pleased with the way he had diverged their information to his sister. But Olan, sadly, doesn't get the expression in his eyes, and so he smiles at Kelly, before tilting his head in Tiana's direction.

Kelly rolls his eyes, and starts walking toward the left side of the court. He gets to the place, and taps the green iron fence, and like pixels spreading itself across the air, the surrounding environment begins to change into a room with a ceiling instead of a sky, and a wall instead of a green iron fence. Kelly had, all this while, been playing tennis inside a simulation.

"Olan, please, help me shut down every system operation in the booth, and make arrangements for our next game. I am certain again I will beat you."

"No, you won't. And be fast." Screams Tiana from outside.

Kelly cringes at her voice, his face bug-eyed and his shoulders raised in bemusement, "She's still around?"

"It appears so, sir."

"Alright, I will be going now. See you later, Olan."

Kelly leaves the facility where he was in, and meets Tiana outside. Tiana sees him approaching, and starts walking toward the main building where they all stay, a building of mainly tinted glass and iron, built with fine structure and design with its edges almost like a polygon shape.

Moments later, they make it into the building, and straight to the dining area, located a few feet from the main living room. White table and chairs with tawny legs, stainless utensils positioned neatly on the table, and a mini staircase that leads to the dining 7-seat dining table. The inside of the home is elegantly lit up with controlled light from the sun outside. Not too bright and not too dim, just enough to give off the beauty that the ultramodern home seeks to portray, also not forgetting that everywhere is made bright by the sun's rays as well.

"Apologies that we are late, mother. Kelly wouldn't leave his game of tennis he was playing, even when he still lost at the end." Tiana tells the mother, settling into her seat.

"After you made me lose." Kelly speaks out, settling into his seat beside his father.

"You were going to lose anyway, the chances were against you. You have never won against Olan."

"Olan is a program, a computer program that I built," he tells her, digging his fork into his salad and eggs and shredded meat, "And so, I have programmed it to beat me always. It reminds me that I am not as good as I think I am."

Tiana scoffs at him begrudgingly, she doesn't utter another word to him as she begins eating her food. She has seen the point of his argument, and knows Kelly is smart enough to actually beat Olan, if he wasn't a computer programme.

"Computers learn and adapt, and Olan has been programmed to learn and shift the dynamic of the game to his standard. This will then–"

"Enough, Kelly," says his mother, "We all know you created Olan to keep you on your toes for your tennis matches, but you do not have to explain to us the intricacies of it all here. Not while you eat." she adds calmly.

Kelly swallows with a guilty expression, he mutters, "My apologies, mother. I just wanted–"

"Another failed etiquette rule, do not speak while eating, and yet, you do it."

"I was already done chewing."

"Not completely."

"And, another break of etiquette, more like manners, not acknowledging mother and father before eating your meal," Tiana interjects abruptly, smirking at Kelly.

Kelly sighs, a spiraling feeling enveloping him and causing his body to go weak. He feels terrible for his actions, for not greeting his father and his mother, for not carrying out the most basic social skill a child ought to do toward his parents, and now, he feels like a failure. To his parents, and especially, to his father.

He slumps into his seat, his face deep and thoughtful, he

says, "Good day, father … Good day, mother. My apologies for not saying this sooner."

The mother, a woman with really dark, short hair and pale skin like creamy lotion, smiles a warm smile. She responds, "It's alright, son. At least, you have retraced your steps, that's what matters at the moment."

But, just as the mother answered, Kelly's father did not respond to his greeting. He only sits there, picking up his meals, and saying nothing. He looks gruff, with dark brown hair and little patches of white hair by the side of his ears, he doesn't look interested in whatever is going on at the table, he doesn't look at anyone and his eyes are still and full of worry.

Kelly and his mother turn their eyes to the man sitting beside them, watching him as he eats his food slowly, and wondering what could possibly be the matter. Tiana takes a look at her father, but quickly looks down at her food. And Kelly's mother puts an expression similar to that of the father, as though she knows what's bothering him.

"Alfred honey, Kelly is greeting you." she tells him.

"I heard." he replies with an unpleasant tone.

Kelly's mother moistens her dry lips with her tongue, a bruised look on her face, she returns to her food with an uncomfortable feeling stirring inside of her.

"Umm, father, I hope everything's fine?" Kelly asks, hoping that he doesn't aggravate his father further.

"Everything's fine."

"Uhh, it doesn't look like this because, since I entered, you haven't been yourself."

Alfred takes up his head to look at Kelly, his eyes scowled in a frown, "Then, how else do you suppose that I should be, Kelly?"

Kelly's mother senses trouble in the air, she turns to Alfred, telling him quickly, "It's alright, honey, you should eat your food now."

"Now, he should answer," Alfred persists, "Since he wants me to be myself, meanwhile, he goes around being other people. Isn't that what you do?" he adds, peering at Kelly in the eye.

He looks at his father with bewilderment, his mind trying to find the pieces and make sense out of it, but can't. He darts his gaze to his mother, but she looks away, and he turns to his sister, only to see someone who probably doesn't care about what's happening. He doesn't stress on it much, as Tiana is sometimes that way.

He lets out a short laugh, "What is all this all about, father? Because I sincerely do not understand. Why the sudden state of outburst?"

Alfred hesitates for a moment, his arms on the table as he searches his son's face, his brows lowered and knit-tight. He exhales as he reclines into his seat, a thoughtful look cloaking his face, he tries to find the words to say to Kelly.

He passes a tongue through his parched lips, he sighs, "You ask me why the sudden state of outburst as though you have no clue of your own actions."

"That's because I don't." He says, looking more confused.

"Of course, you do! You and those Daxonhill people, the way you try to speak with them, play with them, eat their food that isn't even healthy enough, and breathe their unclean air. Don't you know you're exposing yourself to dangers, Kelly?"

"But, you are the one that said I could be going there however I liked, whenever I liked. That I could learn a thing or two from there, why are you saying this now?"

"Well, I made a mistake, and I want you to stop going there."

"No!"

"Yes. There are many other things you stand to benefit here in Anthera, a city that's for you always, and not those hateful, short-minded fellows you are parading with. People who would not even be comfortable around you in the end."

"That is not true, father, not all are that way. And your conclusions are too generic."

"They are generic because they are true. And that girl you walk around with isn't short of them. She is obviously of the same flock as them."

Kelly feels stunned by his father's words, and by the revelation he has just made. He hadn't known he would know about April, or about him going to Daxonhill to see her, to talk with her. But that's the least of his worries, how has he gotten to know, was what Kelly asked himself.

"How did you know about her?" he asks stiffly, slowly, narrowing his eyes at his father.

"Okay, you two stop right now. Right this minute, I don't want anyone to say another word." Says Kelly's mother.

But, her words went unheard as the two men paid no attention to her. Their gazes still fixed on each other, her lips tight and lowered, and their eyes burning with fiery emotions.

"You may be smart, but I am your father, and I know a lot more than you do."

"Are you tracking me?"

"I do whatever is best for my children, and I make sure I know you all are safe. And, this includes girls that aren't suitable for you. Leave her, and focus on your school and career."

"But, I can be focused, and I don't see how she's affecting my life."

"I do not want to believe you have such a small mind not to see the impediments you will be putting yourself through if you continue this. And just like a disease, you must first prevent it, before it spreads and you end up trying to find a cure. So, I will tell you this, Kelly, discontinue whatever mess you have with her, and make Anthera the home for you. There are also–"

"Mess, you call what I have with her a mess. I cannot believe you are the one saying this right now father, and here I was, thinking you were better than this."

Kelly rises to his feet, stepping away from the table and walking away. And when his mother calls him back, he doesn't listen, even when her voice got louder and louder with every call of his name. Kelly gets to the door, slamming it shut with a loud bang against its frame.

Hours later, Kelly is in a hall with his friend, seated with their eyes on a woman speaking to an audience. They are among the audience, and Kelly is surrounded by his four friends at his sides—two are seated beside him and two behind him. This makes it easier for them to communicate without getting side looks or vexed eyes.

The hall is a dim one, lowlights with the only visible person being the speaker. She is a woman of dark skin color, dark, confident eyes, and dark, thick tuft of hair, with plumpy curves and fleshy cheeks. She is wearing a three-piece, dark green suit that clings nicely to her body, speaking to an audience on a topic of inclusivity and community building, about how nations get stronger on all fronts when they are bound together on common grounds and understanding. She speaks eloquently about pontifications, her voice soft and lucid, and every word that falls from her lips sounding like it has been wrapped nicely before coming out.

A few minutes into the lecture, Kelly's friend starts to exchange glances amongst one another, their bright eyes full of questions and confusion. They turn to Kelly, the ones by his side in front, but he doesn't seem to notice them as he keeps his eyes forward, and on the speaker.

One clears his throat, the one with light brown hair on his right, "Should we wait for 3 more minutes before you tell us why you have brought us here, Kelly?"

"Yes, Kelly, we have been here for over 10 minutes now, yet you still haven't told us why we are here. Or, are we here to listen to this lecture?" the one with blond hair on his left asks, his voice sounding exacerbated.

His friends are now complaining, their voices seeping into his ears, unrefined and unconstrained, he feels he isn't doing to let them understand why they have all come here. Kelly then lowers himself into his seat, hesitating to quell his friends' frustration over his action, he thinks of the best reply to furry emotions.

"I had a slight misunderstanding with my father earlier today, and it didn't end well." He tells them.

A sudden quietness befalls them all, bringing a calm amongst them as they all try to find what they can say that would suit Kelly's dilemma.

"What happened?" One behind on the right side of Kelly asks.

"He thinks my going out with April is detrimental to my life as a person," he says slowly, almost as though he was going to cry.

Kelly feels a shifting in the atmosphere, as if his friends agree with his father. He turns to look at them, and finds them having a conformed expression, none is saying anything as they feel Kelly wouldn't be happy with their statement.

"Well, are you guys going to tell me something? Maybe what I can do to convince my father?" he asks them, looking forward to solutions.

But, all Kelly hears is still the speaker's voice, and although she speaks, he feels the room is still empty with a silence that's cutting through his skin. He looks at them again, and starts to get the feeling he is alone on this.

"So, no one will tell me anything, is that?" he asks them, feeling a retching in his stomach.

"It is not like that, Kelly–"

"It's just that, your father might have a point. Maybe, you should do away with that girl, she doesn't need you."

"And, you definitely do not need her."

Kelly instantly starts to regret bringing his friend over to the lecture to discuss a matter such as this, but if there's anything he knows is that, he knows how to properly handle them.

He relaxes into his seat, "Do you know why I brought you all here? To this lecture?"

They all exchange glances with each other, questioning eyes moving from face to the other. No one is able to answer his question, and so they say nothing, though they could see a glaring reason right in front of them.

"No, I, for one, do not," replies the blond haired one.

"The woman on the podium is Sandra Clinton, a professor of Sociology here in Anthera University, and she specializes in the study of societies. So, she knows what it would take for a society to progress, obviously you know her, am I right?"

"That's true. She is one of our greatest minds."

"Good. So, I have brought you all here to show you why my relationship with April might actually be something relating to this, a big change waiting to happen. Me and her, together as one, from two different polarizing groups, we could change the way our societies see each other, ushering in something much…much bigger than all of us. A world where we can all sit under a tree and not get food thrown at us, you get what I am saying?"

His friends all wear thoughtful faces, their gazes on the dark skinned speaker and their ears holding on to all her words. Kelly has given them something to think about, but their fears still persist, Daxonhill folks do not like them — they are the nerds, the presumptuous figures who want nothing but bloated respect, power, and money. That is the way they are viewed, and changing that might present a difficult task for them all.

One sighs, looking at Kelly, "If you think what you are doing is fine and will work out in the end, then, go for it. But know this is your father you are going up against, he can do anything–"

"Don't worry about that, I will handle my father. I only hope you all understand where I am coming from here?"

"Kind of."

"Uhh-hmm."

"I am still processing the various factors involved."

"Just be careful, Kelly. That's all I can say."

Kelly lowers himself into his seat yet again, a smile ripping through his face, content and satisfied, he imagines all he will do once he has gotten the chance for it. And when it seems they are all done talking, their attention shifts to the woman speaking, their bodies relaxed and their minds thinking through the hubris that it had gathered, while pondering on Kelly's words. Certainly, he has given them something to truly think about.

CHAPTER NINE

Kelly is in his room, hunkered down over a bag before him, stuffing into it some clothes that have been neatly placed beside the bag. He is fast-paced, moving as quickly as he could, calculative and fastidious in his thinking, he tries to get the most things he thinks should be with him — or go with him.

As he was with his friends at the lecture hall yesterday, Kelly has decided in himself that he wouldn't be limited by his father, put down on the ground to follow whatever he says. He respects his father, but for the sake of his love for April, he wants to keep a warm, soothing fire alive, between him and April, he is ready to risk it all. Even if it costs him his position in his father's life. This is his way of showing his father he is in-charge, and would do what he deems fit for his life.

As he gets ready, taking things from his shelves and his wardrobe, a device here, a gadget there, and some clothes tucked away in various sections of his wardrobe. So much was his concentration, he didn't realize when someone had entered his room, standing by the door.

"Leaving without saying a word, is that it?" a light, fluid voice speaks out.

Kelly raises his gaze toward the voice, his heart racing against his chest. He sees it's his sister, Tiana, and he stands upright, staring at her as he thinks of what to say.

When Tiana sees he isn't going to say anything anytime soon, she starts walking toward his bed, her expression showing cognizance of what's happening.

"And now that I am here, you still do not want to say a word. Whatever you are doing must be top-secret, am I right?" she asks sarcastically, a smuggish look on her face, "But, of course, if it's top-secret, you wouldn't be sharing it with anyone, hence it defeats its purpose."

Kelly groans with frustration, resuming what he was packing, "I am only going away for a few days, maybe weeks–"

"Or, maybe months even." Tiana cuts in, staring at him with her legs crossed on his bed.

Kelly looks up at her, bemused at how she's able to read his moves, no matter how much he tries to hide it. Kelly has now realized that Tiana possesses the natural discerning wits of their father, able to read the room and find out what they can about something. But, unlike their father, Tiana's can be very frightening, even Kelly himself.

"However, you may see it, Tiana. I can no longer stay in a house where my freedom cannot be guaranteed, and I will be told to do something against my own will. Certainly not, I cannot allow that." He says, scrolling through his phone.

Tiana eases herself down into the bed, "Freedom, you

speak of freedom as it's the reason you are really doing this."

"It is the reason," Kelly snaps, giving a sharp gaze at Tiana.

Tiana looks at him, unperturbed by his knit-tight look, "We all know that's not true, brother. If I must say, father has allowed you more freedom than I could ever have. Yet, you feel you are not given enough because you're disallowed to continue seeing a girl. Now that, brother, is the reason you are doing this."

Kelly, visibly disturbed by his sister's words, zips up his bag, wanting to maintain calmness of mind. He feels his breath stiffening and his chest burning with pain, he tries to imagine other ways this could do for him, so he doesn't get too frustrated.

He puts his bag upright on the bed, shifting his gaze to his sister. He sighs, "I have a question, Tiana."

Tiana arches her brows at her brother, "I don't really like questions, but ask anyway."

He comes over to her and sits beside her, "Have you ever gotten something within your grasp, and you feel this might be like the rest, but you go with anyway. But, at the end, you see something different about that thing you have—"

"Like a programming code you think would be like others, but turns out to be much more than that?"

He snaps his fingers excitedly at her, "There! And then, you feel you are much more happy with it, like you have found something extremely valuable. And then, you start to feel attached to it."

"This feels like a human to human scenario."

"Exactly, Tiana. That is how I feel about the girl I love, I feel she's so different from the others I have seen. Not even Anthera girls can measure up to her personality, like a… like a blend I cannot fully explain."

Tiana stares at him thoughtfully, with a half smile on her face, "Aww, see what love is turning you into. Once a versatile genius, now, look at you, in love and vulnerable. The worst state a human can ever be in."

Kelly jumps to his feet, and straight to his bag, "Ahh, sister, you will never know love till you have felt it, or even tried it."

Tiana folds her face in disgust, "I think I will pass, please."

Kelly laughs heartily, picking up his bag and looping the straps round his shoulder, "So, you won't tell them?"

"I won't," she replies with compassion in her eyes, before it changes to a smuggish one, "Besides, it is always better being an observer than being involved. I would like to see how this plays out, so I won't mention a word of your disappearance to them."

"Good, thank you." Kelly tells her, walking toward the exit.

"But, what if they find you? I mean, father?" Tiana asks, raising her voice a little.

"I already have that taken care of." He tells her, walking out of the room.

Tiana feels an echoing in the room, its emptiness caving in on her. The fact that Kelly isn't here with her, in the room, or in the house, and would be away for a time she doesn't know, makes her feel sullen about it all already. She thinks of it for a while, then slumps into Kelly's bed, she tells herself it will all pass, this loneliness she's already feeling. It will pass.

Few hours later, In Daxonhill, Kelly is with a man, rough looking, a dirty cap over his head, and visible spots of stain on his light brown shirt. The man is old, should be in his early or late 50s, his face riddled with wrinkles, and a pot-belly Kelly keeps questioning himself about. Not like he didn't question other things as well.

They are in an apartment, an apartment Kelly wishes to rent for a few months and for his stay here. The old man has brought him here to show the place, he is the caretaker, and with his looks, Kelly believes the man's body needs more care-taking than the apartment itself.

"What do you think?" the man asks, looking around the apartment, with a content grin on his face.

Kelly's eyes rove through the brown interior of the apartment, he sees the empty sitting room, the dry blue paint of its walls, old and fading. He walks to the kitchen, the dirty and dusty coat over its sink and counters and shelves, the ceilings—they are still intact.

Kelly breathes a sigh of relief, he walks to where the man is standing, managing a smile on his face as the apartment is something worth considering. He thinks it to be a lot better than others, and worth the value of his money since he doesn't have a lot of it. He is his own man, and has the brains to survive in a place like this.

"I think it is alright. I will take it." He tells the old man, looking at him briefly before turning his gaze to the walls of the apartment.

The man grins widely at Kelly, "So, how will you be paying? Cash or bank transfers?"

"Bank transfers, through online banking," Kelly replies, his eyes still roving through the room, with thoughts of a face-lift for it.

The man's brows fall, "Online transfers, hmm…people around here hardly do online transfers, not when you have all these hackers nowadays, people are scared of using it."

Kelly turns to his gaze to the man, "Not when you have your account secured and information about it stored in your head alone. Also, I deal with a reputable bank with good cybersecurity, so my money is sate, I know it."

The man's lips arches downwards, groaning and looking at Kelly with quizzical eyes, "You from around here, boy? Because, you don't seem like it?"

A cold stream of fear grips Kelly throughout his body, he hesitates to answer but knows the after effects of doing such a thing.

He swallows, then turns a feigned smile at the man, "Of course, good sir, I was born and raised here, I am only changing neighborhoods, that's all."

The man narrows his gaze at him, doubtful and full of suspicion, "I don't know, if I didn't know better, I would say you are one of those nerds we often see around. I mean, you've got the hair, the face, even the way you stand on your feet makes you look like them. And your simple dressing too makes me want to believe you are one of them. And now, I am getting the feeling…"

The man walks up to Kelly, standing a few inches close to him and staring at him meanly in the eyes. This grips Kelly in the neck more and more as he finds it suffocating and stifling. Also, the man's stench isn't one he can handle.

"You are lying to me, or are you pretending to be one of them? Like the nerds?" he asks, with a raised brow and a piercing gaze.

Kelly moistens his lips, breathing calmly as the man steps away.

He replies, lying, "You can say that, though I find it very stupid now, to be dressing like them, and walking like them. I don't see anything special about it, just false class and a high sense of worth."

The man grins widely, really widely. He nods his head as he approves of Kelly's statement about the nerds, he says, "That's it, boy. That's what you are supposed to do, their life isn't any better than ours, and we will certainly show them by driving them out of our city forever. You hear me, boy?"

Kelly shudders inside, "Yes…yes, I hear you."

The man's pauses, staring at Kelly thoughtfully, a sly grimace on his face. He soon starts to walk up to Kelly, getting close to his body, this makes Kelly push himself away from touching the man's clothes or inhaling any more bad stench.

"With the way you look, you don't seem like the one who would have it hard with the ladies. Just make sure you don't overdo things, or act like you're smart, girls here don't like that. That is why they don't like nerds in the first place. So, instead of dressing all high and classy, like you know it all, be more in-line with your Daxonhill self, and just flow. You hear me?"

Kelly nods quickly, hoping in his mind that the man steps away soon. Which he does anyway. He lets out a laugh, and starts to make for the door, and as he walks on, Kelly thinks about what he has said and what it could mean for him and April, the effects of it. He decides to see how it goes, and whether April is that type of girl, though she hasn't shown it to him, hence that personality he still can't figure out yet.

"Don't forget my money, boy," the man reminds him as he walks through the door, laughing to himself, "Online bank transfers, wait till they hit ya." He adds, chuckling and shutting the door.

Kelly's brows shoot up, a realization hitting him, "I didn't even get to know his name. Huhh, oh well, I guess it's till next time then."

***

Over at Daxonhill High, that same afternoon, humid and slightly windy, with the sun hovering lazily in the sky.

April is in the library, books piled up one atop the other, a laptop beside her, and a textbook and an exercise book right in front of her. She is scribbling something in it, her eyes running through the textbook, searching for needed information and once that has been gotten, she turns her focus to the exercise book and writes it down.

It has been 2 weeks since she and Nigel started work on their project, and a lot has been done and covered that April feels relieved about it, about finishing in time and delivering one of the best presentations her class and the school has ever seen. Anytime she thinks about it, it gives her a pleasant feeling in her belly, rising up to her heart, causing it to beat with glee. A smile would tease the edges of her lips, and she would hold it back, sensing that someone is probably looking at her, even when that's unlikely to happen.

Moments later, Nigel walks into the library and takes his seat beside April, watching her intently while she works. She pretends as though she doesn't see him and this makes him smile.

"You are early today," April breaks the silence between them.

"Thanks for noticing, I know today is the day we often meet, so I made sure I do not miss it for anything." He replies with a charm in his voice.

April turns a side glance at him, "Hmm, that's okay, I guess."

"Yeah," Nigel says, a feeling of uncertainty and sense of duty setting in within him.

He taps his fingers on the table, a means to distract himself a little from the discomforting vacuum he feels expanding between them. He thinks for a moment, looks at April as reads through the book, and thinks to himself to do something at least. He hasn't been much of a help to her lately, in researching, in writing and compiling, and in adding necessary information to what she has already got. And he was tired of being a thorn in her skin, a pesky insect buzzing on and on in her face and in her ears, an insect she would always try to push away. He was tired of that too.

Nigel lets out a restive sigh, sinking into his chair, and twirling his lips round his face, thinking, what should he do?

"I have got something for you, wanna see it?" Nigel tells her, unsure if it will yield anything. Yet, he tries.

Her eyes still focused on the book, "Yeah, what is it?"

He straightens himself in the chair, and digs his hand into his pocket. He takes out a sheet of paper, a folded piece of paper, and hands it to April. He searches her face for an expression that would show dissatisfaction in her, that she doesn't appreciate his input in what they are doing.

She takes the paper and wonders what could be in it. She stares at it curiously, asking herself what it might be or what it could have. And just as she hesitated collecting it, it takes a while before she eventually starts opening it up. She gets it open, and sees that it contains the works of their project, the animals and their period of existence, what they fed on, and how they survived. Works that she had already written, except for one animal she hasn't written yet — the megalania. She feigns a smile, partly true in its composition, "This is great, Nigel, it will help in our work. I will make use of it as soon as I find the periods the mammoths and the titanoboas existed. I have been having a rough time looking for them."

"Oh," exclaims Nigel, "Well, have you searched for it online? You know, you can never go wrong searching for it online."

April gives him an unpleasant stare, "You think if I haven't done that, I would be telling you that. I have already searched online, and I still can't find anything. I don't know what I am doing wrong."

"What about the books here? There are a lot of them, surely you would see it." Nigel suggests.

April sighs exhaustively, "I have, though not all. Please, help me check."

Nigel, glad that he is finally lending a hand, helping April out the way she would like, he takes a book from one of the piles on the table and he starts flipping through it. He tries to pay as much attention as he can, eager to find something, something relating to the problem April's facing. That way, she would be proud of him, happy that he can be there when he needs to, and he can finally get the chance to keep making her happy.

After minutes of frantic efforts, pages checked, sites after sites opened and read through, April and Nigel slump into their seats feeling exhausted and confused about their work. They had not anticipated that an impasse would be met this way, causing them to overthink a solution to no avail.

'Where could it possibly be?' April asks herself as she stares at the ceiling, still not able to figure the problem.

Nigel, however, doesn't see the need to bother himself about it, he could just leave it if he were the one, but doesn't know if April would take that path too. April hasn't always been the type to convince easily, but she is lazy, that he knows quite well.

He turns to face her, "Well, we have tried, April, if we can't find the year the mammoths and that other animal existed, then, we leave it."

"They are important in the work as well, and I really need them in our work."

Nigel shrugs, "They shouldn't be that important, are they? I mean, you can just leave them without writing anything on them."

"I have already written something on them, erasing that whole work now will put me behind time, and I don't want that."

"There are other animals you can use, right? Just erase the mammoth and that other animal I can remember–"

"The titanoboa."

"Right, the titanoboa or something, and just use other animals. I did see some that weren't in our work, and I saw their periods of existence, so…I don't know."

April lets out a breath of exhaustion, she props her body upright and gets to her feet, slowly as she does it, and then, she comes to a pause.

She turns a tired gaze at Nigel, speaking slowly, "I have already done a lot of work on these two animals, and erasing them will be difficult. So, I can't, Nigel, I will just find a way to get the dates or we won't add the dates at all. Either way, they stay, and I am going to get something to eat."

"I am coming with you." Nigel days to her, getting out of his with so much vigor and zest, hyped by April's presence near him. Though he knows she doesn't notice that now, he believes she will some day.

After school, and on her way home, April digs for her phone in her bag, and places a call to Kelly. She has been thinking of her project, her mind hasn't been kind to her since she saw the problem, unable to understand why it isn't on the internet or in any of the books she and Nigel have searched through.

Kelly was what she thought would be her saving net, to help navigate the internet better than her, and also the fact that he's a nerd. So, he should be able to help. The call goes through, and it rings for a while, but no one picks up. She dials it again, but no one picks up still. She dials it for the third time, almost seething through the eyes, and the same thing happens. She groans, her mind close to exploding to bits, she plunges her phone back into her back pocket.

"Why aren't you picking up, Kelly?" she asks herself, imagining the possible things he could be doing.

CHAPTER TEN

Damien moves from room to room, opening doors and peaking into them, searching for something or someone. When he couldn't find what he was looking for, he goes trotting downstairs and straight to the kitchen, he peers round the corners of the room, he sighs when he couldn't find anything. He goes to the back of the house, and onto the lawn, and he groans when he still couldn't find any-thing. A thought crosses his mind, and he runs excitedly into the house, grinning and panting, and moments later, he walks out through the front porch of their home.

"So, this is where you are. I have been looking for you for a while now," he says, walking toward April and sitting next to her. She turns to look at him, she's sitting on the little stairs of the house, with a book in hand, and the gentle flow of the evening wind caressing against her skin. She takes her gaze, turning it toward the street, "Why are you looking for me? Besides, I have been here."

Damien's lips bends inward, "Well… you are often in your room, if not there, then, up at the attic doing whatev-er you do there—"

"That's my thinking space."

"And, I guess you have turned our front porch to your thinking space as well? Maybe your room isn't enough anymore."

April gets annoyed, turning to him with lowered brows, "What do you want, Damien? As you have seen, I was busy."

Damien crosses his legs on the stairs below him, looking down at his feet, "I am sorry, I didn't mean to make you upset."

"It's alright, but seriously, what do you want?" April asks him, as she feels she has really been disturbed.

Damien sighs, "I and your friend saw today, on my way to school."

April's heart sinks to her stomach, it skips a beat as she imagines who this friend could be. A lot of questions start racing through her mind, and she hopes the friend isn't the one she's thinking of.

"Which friend?" she asks sternly.

"Reilly, of course," he replies, lessening April's worries, "Which other friend do you have, if not her."

Damien sighs loudly, and April, her sigh was inward, closing her eyes in relief as her fears didn't come to pass. Had it been him, she would have called him, and told him off, warning him not to come visit her ever again. She would also think him to be a stalker, calling her on her line, coming to her, and now, her home. That wouldn't allow it.

"Okay, what about her?" she asks, her chest feeling lighter than before.

"I tried greeting her today, and she treated me like I was a boy, a little boy. When I said hello to her, she tapped my hair and told me how much I have grown, speaking to me like I was her little brother." Damien laments with an exacerbated breath.

April smiles widely, almost laughing, "Aren't you her little brother? I mean, you are just 12, and Reilly is like 16? I told you, she's older than you."

"And, I said love knows no boundaries. It is not fair seeing your crush treating you like a baby brother, when I should be treated like another guy. An older guy."

"Hmm," April thinks for a moment, holding back a laugh, "Life is truly unfair, to you and to me, even when you're just 12 years old, crushing on your senior. You know that won't happen, not today, not ever."

"That's unfair," he says with stormy eyes full of pain, looking at April.

"As I said, life's unfair, Damien. And you just have to deal with it however you see it. Also, here comes Reilly now."

Damien turns swiftly to the direction April is pointing, his eyes wide open with consternation in them as he sees Reilly walking over to them. He makes it stand but can't, his mind wants to, but his body can't. And the longer he stays there, sitting there, the closer Reilly gets to their front lawn.

From a few feet away, Reilly smiles an open-lipped smile at them, waving her hand in the air as she approaches. April waves back happily, relaxed and unconstrained, but Damien waves at her with his nerves wrecking at every point in his body. He suddenly feels hot where he sits, the cool breeze outside having very little to do against his skin, his heart immediately hating where he is and how he is unable to get up and move.

"You are unusually happy today, hmm, Reilly." April says to her, grinning from ear to ear.

"I believe I have the right to always be happy, no matter what, right?" Reilly asks, standing before April and Damien.

"Yeah, that's right. Anyways, I didn't see you after school, what happened?"

Reilly beats her hand against the air, speaking in a high-pitched voice, "Oh, that's a long story, I will tell you. Hey, Damien."

Damien feels himself turning into a pool of himself, Reilly's voice heating up his body in ways even he doesn't understand. He tries frantically to get up to his feet and go inside, but he still can't find the strength to do it.

"Hey, Reilly, how…how are you doing?" he says to her, managing a reply.

"I'm good," she replies, turning her gaze to April again, "Do you know I saw him earlier this morning, on his way to school with your dad?"

"No, I didn't," April lies, grinning very widely.

"Well, I saw him today, and felt like he is going to grow up to be a very tall, fine young man. The girls are going to crawl and grubble all over him. Just look at him, small, yet promising."

April looks at Damien still face, smiling, "You don't say."

They both laugh. Annoyed, Damien gets up and walks out of there, causing Reilly to stop laughing, wondering what went wrong.

She reverts her gaze to April, "What just happened? Did I do anything wrong?"

April waves the issue aside, "Ohh, it's just Damien and one of his troubled moments, he will come around."

Reilly shrugs it off, sensing she hasn't done anything to make Damien upset. When, in fact, her statement had upset him, making remarks that made him like a child was insulting to him, at least, that's the way he saw it, and it bothered him. And, coming to terms that she regarded him as a kid brother, instead of something farther than that, hurt his feelings too, and all those strength he had lost staring at her, came back, with not a single atom of it missing.

Reilly walks up to where April sits, replacing Damien where he was sat. She looks down at April's laps, "You are reading a book, what kind?"

April takes up the book at face level, "Yeahhh, this is Stacy Quinn's Finding Your Way Out Of The Murky Waters Of Shallowness. It's a 250 page book, divided into 18 parts, and I just started reading it today. It's a good book, and… why are you looking at me like that?"

Reilly groans, rolling her eyes, "Why will you be reading this book? Do you even need it? Or, is it because of that nerd?"

April knits her brows together in a frown, pushing her body backwards in confusion and subtle disgust, "No! This is not for anyone, and certainly not for him. No! For the love of good things, why would you think that, Reilly?

"Because, only nerds read books, and the last time, I checked you are not a nerd, April." Reilly replies, raising her voice slightly in a cynical manner.

April turns her face to the front, looking elsewhere, "Well, not only nerds read, Reilly, even we have to read."

"Not this!" says Reilly, pointing at the book, "Why would you want to find your way out of a murky water, hmm, April? Do you think your life is such a mess, that you would want to change it? I don't know, maybe change it into something else, like clean water, or an ocean with a rainbow at the end, hmmm, April? Is that it?"

Reilly's tone is starting to get haughty and raspy, with every word hitting against April's ears like a sharp, pointed knife pushed in to make her bleed.

April knows Reilly wouldn't understand stuff like this, she wouldn't even want to understand, and trying to make her see things differently would be like adding water to an ocean. It will make no difference to her.

April watches as their neighbors pass, almost all of them are smiling and she envies them and their little world, wanting to live in this little world of theirs. She turns to Reilly, she looks pained, but she is often this way, always cautioning her about the nerds, trying to talk her out of doing some things or talk her into doing some things. Either way, they are all in the negative and geared toward hating the nerds more, and sadly, she isn't such kind of person.

"I am sorry, Reilly," April says after some moments of silence, "I am sorry that I cannot be that friend who can share in the same thing as you do, or who can say mean words to the very people that help us shape the world we live in. I am sorry for not being that friend, but I hope you get to understand that there are some things much bigger than us, things we can't understand–"

"Oh my, you have started sounding like them too," she says in awe and surprise, looking at April queerly.

"Whatever, just know that this is for me, and I am only trying to know and understand myself. And, if this is–"

"How else do you understand yourself, and to what extent? For all I know, you are good to me this way, why don't you understand that, April?" Reilly cries out, pleading with April.

""I don't know, Reilly," she replies sullenly, looking down at the book and its inscriptions, her eyes laden with emotion, "I just don't know."

***

The next day, a Saturday, with no school to be running

to in the morning, April and Damien work through their chores for the morning, getting them done as fast as they could. As soon as they are done, April gets herself to leave the house, the incident of yesterday still recurring in her mind and she finds it very unpleasant to have around. So, she has decided to go into the city, and make herself comfortable to forget it all.

The thought that she would be able to find relative peace in something else, reinforces her idea about stepping out of the house. And, she is usually not an outdoor person, as she only goes out when Reilly comes around or when she's been sent out to get groceries or pick up something for her mom. Or, just like today, to go clear her mind and rechannel whatever tempest is taking place in her head. Yesterday hadn't been pretty, not with Reilly walking out on her.

She goes into the living room as she is all dressed and ready to leave.

"Hey, mom, I am on my way to the mall. I will be back very soon." She tells her mother, dressed in a blue hoodie and a blue jean trouser, with a pair of black sneakers to go with her outfit.

Her mother, watching the television in the sitting room, turns her attention to April, though she isn't looking at her, "Okay, dear, who are you going with? Reilly? Tell her I say hello."

April wears a brooding face, looking toward the front door, "No, mom, I am not going with Reilly today. It's just me."

Dareen looks at her with a befuddled mien, her mouth

agape, "What?! What happened? I thought it is always you two, together when you are going out? Is she sick?"

April starts to get comfortable with the questions, "No, mom, she has the thing she's doing, and won't be able to join me, that's why."

"Oh, okay," says the mother, fixing her gaze back at the television, "If you see her, tell her I say hi anyway."

"Alright, mom," she says, walking toward the door.

""Can I come alone?" asks Damien in a low, wounded tone, "You know, since she won't be joining you and all, maybe I can fill her space, you know."

April looks at her brother thoughtfully, trying to consider his request. But, after much thought, she sees his coming along as a little bit of an inconvenience. She turns him down, though sad about it.

Damien shrugs his shoulders, going to sit in the sitting room, "It's alright, maybe next time then, right?"

"Right."

April pays a visit to one of her most favorite spots or shops in Daxonhill, the arcade shop where she can play whatever games she wishes. She enters the building and marvels at how much the place has changed since she last came. And that was a year ago. And though, there are now new arcade machines, new game sets like a virtual reality motorcycle racer, which April says she would ride one day, and another game set with joysticks and goggle-like headset the people seem to be wearing now.

The place is crowded and noisy, the sounds of cheering voices rising up to the air, the blue tinted room giving it a better welcoming environment for everyone who wishes to play. And also, because the owner had installed blue lights and tinted their windows a little darker, this was meant to make their customers' gaming experience better and more satisfying. And judging from the cheers and grinning faces, they achieved their aim.

Though, this is unnerving for April. She isn't used to having this many people around. The arcade shop wasn't always like this, it usually had few people playing games, but now and with the new game sets, the place is more boisterous than before. And she hopes no one is at her own favorite arcade machine.

As the thoughts hit her, she hurried her steps to the aisle where it is located.

'Hope they haven't moved it, or worse, people might be there. Ohhh, no…' she says as she starts to panic.

She gets to the aisle, and with slow movement, she peeks through a corner, and sees only a person there. He is playing the game as well, and April feels relieved by it all. She sighs a breath of refreshed relief.

She begins to walks the fellow, slowly and with an intention to tell the person she will be next after him. But, as she gets closer, she begins to reduce her steps, watching closely and inquisitively, her brows furrowing as she thinks where she had seen him before.

'He looks familiar, a lot more familiar than I would know. Ahh, I am not in the mood to see anyone who I know, could it be Nigel? Ohh, please, no.' she says to herself, still peering at the tall figure whose face is hidden in the hood of his hoodie.

She walks closer to her right, the angle where the person stands, and the brightness from the arcade machine illuminates his face to the point that she sees him clearly now.

Her heart skips and turns in her chest, hammering against it heavily that she feels it might leap out from her mouth, down to the tiled floors. Gripped with fear, she turns around and starts walking toward the end of the aisle, fast and stiff are her steps that a rat would pass and she wouldn't notice it. She gets to the corner and makes a turn when she feels a hand grab her from behind. She gasps and turns her gaze, and meets a set of two blue eyes staring at her. Her world suddenly comes to a stop.

"April, I knew you were the one." Kelly says to her, his teeth out behind a smile.

April manages a smile, "Kelly, I didn't see you there. What a pleasant surprise."

"It really is, isn't it," he tells her, "I wouldn't have seen you either, but when I saw you walking away, I just knew you were the one. If you noticed, there's this sway you give to your hips when you walk, very distinct to you alone." Kelly further adds.

"Oh," she says, feeling somewhat embarrassed by it, "I haven't noticed."

"Ohh, it's alright, not everyone notices anyway. Come on, wanna play fruit martial? I was this close to beating your score, then I saw you, and I lost the game. But with you playing by my side, I will know how good I am."

April puts her hands behind her, fiddling with them, "Ahh, I don't know, I think I have got—"

Kelly takes her by the hand, cutting her mid-sentence, "Come on, it will be fun, trust me. Or, don't you like your game again?"

She allows herself to be dragged by Kelly, to be pulled as though she needed what would be shown to her. She doesn't need it, she would have walked out if Kelly hadn't held her from behind.

But, that is, it's Kelly that's the problem, the air around him, the smile on his face, the words he uses, the way he speaks, his chummy personality are what draws her to him.

Looking at him makes her feel comfortable, maybe beyond comfortable. She feels she could stay with him as long as she likes, it pleases her to see him, to talk with him, to have him to talk to her.

It makes her feel great, somewhat powerful and seen, and she loves whatever she gets standing beside him, as she has never gotten a feeling such as this before, not with other boys, no.

"Okay, I have restarted the game, and here's your own shooter." Kelly says, handing her shooter.

April takes the shooter from him with a near trembling hand, steadying herself to be able to play the game at least.

Kelly positions himself as well for the game, his hands clasped around the trigger. He looks at April, and sees she is also set to play the game, and a compassion smile escapes from his lips.

"Are you ready to lose?" he asks her, looking at the screen as it counts down.

April smiles. She says nothing as she raises her shooter to the screen.

The game begins, and the two starts trying to defeat the other. Their keen eyes on every fruit that pops out, tearing it to shreds with their shooters in a race to victory. April is paying acute attention to the fruits as they emerge from below the screen, taking them out as quickly as she can, and watching the timer and the number of fruits she has shot already.

Kelly is also paying rapt focus at his side of the game, his eyes on his timer and the total amount of fruits he has taken out. He tries to avoid obstacles as much as he can, shooting only the fruits that appear as fruits.

Few minutes later, the game ends, and they both lower their shooters to their sides, looking at the screen with wide eyes.

"Well, I guess I still have what it takes, hmm, April?" Kelly says to her, a grin creaking through his face.

"Don't get too happy, Kelly, I will get you next time. Take it from me, it's a promise."

Kelly laughs with a sonorous undertone to his laughter,

folding his hands around his chest, "If you say so, I shall await that time."

April stares at him for a moment, her eyes looking at the smallness to his nose, the length of it becoming clear to her now that she hadn't noticed before. How slanted it looks and small it looks, and how well rounded the side to his eyes are, and his cheeks are smooth and shiny, one could mistake it for a baby's skin. And his eyes, she loves his eyes, the blueness of it, looking like a deep blue sea that she can go swimming in. Every second she stands staring at him makes her unwilling to move, as she feels entangled with his being already.

And just like April, Kelly feels the same as well, though he still has his doubts, and hopes this is all not a hoax. The worst thing that could possibly happen to him is to be chasing after a shadow in a dark room, as he knows where he would end up. A deadend.

Kelly swallows, breaking away from April's gaze. April looks away as well, feeling a bit embarrassed for holding on to his gaze for that long, moving and kicking her legs into the air to mitigate the shame swirling in her.

Kelly asks, "What about your friend? You didn't bring her alone."

April looks around as though looking for Reilly. She replies, "Yeah, ahh, she didn't come with me today, she's not…she's not around."

She hesitated in her reply, unsure if to say what she has in mind or not.

Kelly nods his head, "Oh, it's alright, I guess. At least, I am safe today, and I get to have you all to myself."

His statement makes April smile tenderly at him. He sees it, and feels he's doing something right. He then decides to push it a bit further.

"How about we go get a drink, what do you think? I am starving."

"Hmm," April thinks for a moment, "Alright, I am starving as well too."

Kelly laughs, then gestures to her to walk first, playing the perfect gentleman role to her. She smiles and starts walking in front, with him behind her.

"So, where do you think we should go? Any thoughts?" He asks, walking beside her.

"I don't know. Know any place?"

Kelly grins as he stares into the distance, "I have got just the right place."

CHAPTER ELEVEN

"And for how long do you intend to be like this?" says Kelly's mom in their immaculate minimalist living room.

She is watching her husband walk back and forth in a corner in the living room, close to the stairs that lead to the dining area. He isn't looking too pleased about something, scowled brows, tight-lipped, eyes pensive and seething with anger, or maybe worry, but more of angry nevertheless. His hands are behind him, clasped together in each other as he paces the floor of the living room, momentarily stopping in his steps to think, and then continuing once his thoughts elude him.

His wife, her face writhe with worry, follows him with her gaze, tilting her head wherever he goes. She heaves her chest, sighing out a restive breath. She stands to her feet, and with elegance in her steps, walks to her husband, to calm his pulses, she thought. Something she contemplates she would try.

"Alfred, you need to stop hurting yourself over something like this. It will yield no result, and her heart will be at risk of an attack." She says with a soothing, compassionate tone.

"I'm healthy, thank you." He tells her stiffly, leaving her

side as he continues pacing the floor.

She groans with frustration clouding her mind and her eyes, she holds his hand again when he crosses her path. She carries her hands to his face, staring into his dark brown eyes with a soft smile on her face.

She tells him, "I believe, whenever he may be, he is safe. He is a smart boy, and surviving wouldn't be a problem for him. So please, come and sit, and let me bring you some fruits, you have overworked your heart already."

Alfred looks into her face for a moment, his eyes dilating at the presence of his wife's touch. The tightness to his lips starts to loosen, so do his eyes as they start to calm. He begins to feel himself coming to a place of inner peace, his wife. But, that only lasted for a few minutes, as his lips falls again in rekindled anger, grunting and brushing himself free from his wife's hold

"You do not listen." cries out his wife.

"No, Geneva, it is Kelly that doesn't listen," he bellows, standing to face her, "Why would he leave this house, leave the city, and wander off to a place I cannot find. That we don't know. Why?!"

"I am sure he is safe."

"How do we know that? And besides, his safety isn't my problem, my problem is him being influenced wrongly by the wrong people. And I wonder, what does he find in them?"

"It may not be them, Alfred honey, more like her. Also,

he is grown up already, so let him spread his wings as wide as he can."

"And, I suppose that includes hacking into my systems, and disabling his tracking ID in it. He has erased everything that makes it possible to find him, and that…and that makes me so angry."

Geneva rolls her eyes, the side of her right lip raises in a half smile. She folds her arms, "Reminds me of someone who hacked into our security cameras just to watch me sometimes. Sounds very familiar, if you ask me."

"Whatever," he says, dismissing Geneva's statement, "He isn't picking my calls or returning any of my texts. I have tried to track his phone, but Olan told me Kelly has input in it some sort of firewall that makes it impossible to perforate its protocols. What sort of rubbish is that?" he asks, exasperated.

Geneva gives up, and walks to a living room couch to have a seat, "That sounds like the kind of rubbish you would do. Our son's own is no different."

"In that case, I shall show him what madness really is," Alfred says, walking to the centre of the living room. He gets to the glass table placed in the middle, and he picks up his phone.

He dials Kelly's number, it rings the first time, but he doesn't pick. He dials it again, and it goes off abruptly. He groans, and places the call again, and this time, Kelly takes the phone call.

"Why haven't you been picking your calls? And where

are you? You haven't been at home for 2 weeks now, where are you right this minute?" He demands with a thunderous, raspy tone.

Kelly sighs on the other end, "And if I tell you where I am, what would you make of that? I suppose you will send some of your men to come find me, tie me up, and bring me back home, isn't it?"

Alfred hesitates to answer, he looks over at Geneva with a thoughtful gaze before switching attention back to Kelly, "Kelly, you need to understand that…this is not the life you should be living. You can have more, you can be more, and with your type of character and charm, girls here will love you the way you want. I see no reason for you to–"

"I am happy here, father, and there's nothing you can do about that."

"Which is why I am saying to you, consider your choices, or the consequences of your actions now will marr your later future. And, you do not want that. You know I only want the best for my children, for you."

"I wish that was right, father. I really do, because no matter how much I look at it, I always see the wrong your best embodies. It isn't the best that stems from what we want, but what you want and see, it all stems from the inner part of your selfishness, the image you want to preserve. That is where all this is coming from, not you wanting the best for us."

Alfred walks over to a couch, sitting on it with calmness of mind, as though not disturbed by Kelly's words. He relaxes into it, "But, don't you think you would be wasting years of your life on the wrong thing, nurturing it till maturity, only to see it die right in front of you? That is, if it reaches maturity even."

Kelly laughs at the other end, "I believe I know where this is coming from, what if she doesn't like me? What if all I have been doing is in vain, and I am just expending my energy for nothing? What if? … What if? And yet, I am together with her, what do you make of that?"

His father narrows his eyes as his hands start to quiver in anger, he lets out a sigh in a show of restraint, "And what if you are with her? What difference does it make? She's a Daxonhill girl, and you, a boy from Anthera. A nerd. The brain behind their perceived slavery, the usurper of their wealth, using his technology and brilliance to gain advantage over them. Isn't that how they see you?"

Kelly doesn't answer, hesitating a reply as his father smirks at his own statement. He could imagine how Kelly would be feeling at the moment, the look on his face, the anger, the fact that he knows his father is saying the truth. The silence he keeps makes his father wear a wide smug smile on his face, content his words are having the needed effect he wanted them to have.

"However you look at it, father, I am resolute in my action, and I will make sure I see that this doesn't die. I have given it a lot of thought, and I have finally decided I will push through with it."

Alfred bites his lips, still trying to restrain himself from an emotional outburst. He calms himself, sounding settled, "At least, come home so we can see you. Do that for us as your parents, your mother is worried sick about you."

Geneva shifts on the couch, twisting her face and whispering to herself, "I am not worried sick at all. I am actually fine."

Alfred looks at her with a wicked, piercing gaze. She sees it and shifts on the couch again, showing reluctance to comply with Alfred's games, as she sees it.

"Well, mother can wait. I will be back when I feel like coming back. So, if you would excuse me, I have a beautiful Daxonhill girl to go back to. Thank you, father."

His father's face becomes heavy with chaotic and rigid emotions, fierce and glaring that his eyes become misty with held back anger and bitterness. Alfred begins to regret letting his son go out into Daxonhill at an early age of his life, he thought he was young and needed to explore a little bit, as Kelly was once a shy and timid boy.

He didn't know he would ever grow up to defy his orders, renegading on his rules. Though, at 18, that was the usual thing for boys his age, to be stubborn, but he thought he would know better, and do things the right way. Kelly is smart after all, but he was wrong. He was utterly mistaken.

"Worried sick, you say, you really need to do better," Geneva tells him, bringing in some life into the deepening silence that was in the room.

Alfred takes up his gaze at her, stern and rigid, "Why do I get a feeling you are encouraging this aberration, aiding him on his way to self-deterioration. Why?"

Geneva's face shrivels in surprise, changing the way she had crossed her legs, "Aiding his way self-deterioration?

Really, Alfred? Weren't the one that said you could keep going to Daxonhill even when I was against it, that it was for learning purposes, you said. And now, I am okay with what he has become, you want to cook me alive for that?"

"That's what I mean?"

"So, what do you mean, hmm, Alfred? Because, I don't understand."

"I am just saying you ought to help me out here, to help me convince him of the folly he is riding on. You and I know his future cannot be built with that girl, whoever she may be, he needs concentration and time to focus. He isn't even going for his business mastership class anymore, how does he run my company with such a lackadaisical mind?"

"But, we also know he has a great mind, and can obviously cope with the path he has taken. Let's just see it as him multitasking."

"Multitasking?"

Geneva shrugs, hoping she was convincing enough.

"You know what, Geneva?" he asks, standing up, "If he is not going to come home, I will go bring him home myself. I cannot sit idly by, and watch my own son roam in a darkness he created himself, or I helped him create. I just can't." Alfred tells his wife, storming out of the house.

Geneva gets up as well, walking behind him, "Hope it is not what I am thinking? Alfred, you are going to put yourself in a lot of health risk doing this, you need to stop."

Alfred doesn't answer her, his mind distant and latched on another line of thought. He walks to his car, gets it open, and enters inside. Geneva joins him seconds later, still talking and going unheard and unanswered, yet she still speaks. He hits the ignition, and the car comes alive with a slight jerk, humming a sound. A while later, he drives away from the premises, gripping the steering wheel tighter than he could realize.

At the same time Alfred and Geneva are leaving their house to come find Kelly in Daxonhill, Kelly and April are in a restaurant he had brought them to. A place he had seen and fallen in love with since he moved to the city. The food had drawn him once, he likes the fact they served highly nutritious meals, something he could eat and not add weight. But later on, he falls in love with the environment, the interior and the friendly ambience it has.

He likes that people come here and share high quality time with others, without much noise and fuss, almost as if it was built by a nerd, for nerds. He doesn't know the owner, yet, but if he does, he would shake the person's hand for a job well done.

However, Kelly thanks the cashier at the counter where he picks up food, and saunters his way back to April. Arriving seconds later with two trays of cheese sandwich, two cups of smoothie, a salad for Kelly, and two hamburgers. He smiles at April, who returns it back, as he takes his seat.

"Sorry that took so long, I was caught with something." He apologizes, setting the trays he brought with him.

"It's no problem, I figured that, maybe you had something important you were discussing over the phone. You looked angry in a way." She tells him.

Kelly tries to cover his pain with a smile, he says, "Yeah, it was…err, just a little misunderstanding I had with a person. But, I am sure he will come to his senses soon."

"Oh," exclaims April, looking curious, "Was it with a friend?"

"Errr," Kelly thinks for a moment, sifting his mind for an answer, "Yeah, a friend. It was a friend. I was trying to make him see reasons why what he thinks may not be what it really is, like a shift in perspective, you know what I am saying?"

April looks at her food with a thoughtful gaze shrouding her eyes, a thought crossing her mind and she starts to feel Kelly's situation may just be similar to hers in some ways, if not all.

She extends her hand to take her hamburger, "Yeah, I guess I do. I am equally having the same problems with my own friend. Wish it could end in some way, or make her see things a bit more differently. It's draining anytime I think of it."

Kelly stares into her still eyes, feeling drawn to it as she lowers her gaze to the table top, clear and vibrant, like the stars he studies in his astronomy class. Her expression is calm and gentle, tender to the view, and he wishes he could take her face in his hands and feel them even for a millisecond, to be close to her like her hair is to her face. He suddenly envies the hair, how they can touch her face and he can't, wishing he could be a strand among them.

Alfred and Geneva are still on their way to Daxonhill, and are now on the highway leading to the basic people town. Alfred still doesn't bat an eye at Geneva's words, no matter how she emphasizes it. Yet, she doesn't stop talking and he regrets allowing her to join him. But, how couldn't he? She would just follow him with her own car, and it's bad enough she's here with him, in his own car, having her follow him will only annoy him further.

"And here you are, complaining that your sin doesn't listen. Yet, I am trying my best to make you stop your rash action, and you still persist, where do you think he got that from?"

"Would you please let me drive? I am trying to concentrate." He tells her in a gruff tone, his eyes on the road.

"From you, of course, where else?" she answers her own question, "And you think he will listen to you? That's a very odd thing to expect, if not difficult even."

"I am trying to drive here, Geneva."

Geneva looks at him with a stiff face, eyes narrowed, "Well, drive slowly, you are about to cross the speed limit for this road. You need to be at 70 miles per hour, and where are you? … Close to a hundred miles per hour! Alfred, please, slow down, at least, keep us alive till we reach Daxonhill. You don't want any accidents, do you?"

"Nothing will happen, we will be fine."

"Says the man driving at a.hundred miles per hour, you are going to get us killed."

He turns to her, fed with her words, "Will you keep quiet for once, you have been talking since we started this trip, and you don't seem to want to stop. I have a son to go and save, and the only thing you have been doing is blab and blab about consequences and how wrong my approach is."

"That's because they are wrong, Alfred."

"Well, I don't want a word from you again." He commands.

"Well, father, that's no way to treat a woman," says Tiana, showing up instantly behind them.

Startled by Tiana's sudden appearance, Alfred and Geneva scream and jerk in their seats, as their hearts explode in a burst of panic attacks and cold shivers coursing down their spines and all over their bodies. Alfred loses control of the car for a moment, but soon steadies its track on the road, followed closely by curses and yellings from drivers outside.

"Tiana, what have you been doing back there? And how did you enter the car? You nearly killed, twice even." Geneva asks her with a heavily thrumming heart.

"My apologies, mother, I didn't know I haven't been noticed yet, I felt you all knew, but kept quiet, so I decided to come up and stop hiding. The story of how I got here? Well, that will be discussed some other time, I believe." Tiana tells het, seeming unfazed about the tension in the car.

Alfred still trying to steady his own breath, "Regardless of whatever circumstances that may have led to your hiding in the car, and scaring us like that, you are—"

"Grounded, for 6 months, perhaps. I knew that would follow too, I was expecting it." Tiana completes her father's words.

"And yet, you took the risk of coming." Says Geneva, looking at her shoulder.

Tiana shrugs at her mother's words, "I like to take my chances."

Geneva grunts at her daughter's defiance, the nonchalance to her character and the way she trivializes things. Tiana has always been like that, or not, she was a meek kind of girl in her earlier years of 7 and 8. Then, she started to change at 10, and now, 13 and full of insights about a lot of things, Tiana approaches life a lot differently from them. Almost as though, she doesn't care about consequence, like she's experimenting. And, such a thought scares both of them.

"Do both of you know where Kelly would even be? I feel like you are just entering the city without a clue as to where he might be," Tiana tells them.

Alfred brows knit together in a guilty grimace, tightening his hold on the steering wheel, "You are right, we don't know. But, if there is anything we know, or I know is that, he is with the girl, perhaps in a restaurant, or mall, or a park, or wherever teenage lovers go to hang out."

Tiana peers at him closely, with mocking eyes, "Okay, but where exactly? That's the crux, I believe you don't know, father."

Alfred and Geneva exchange side glances, their expression showing that their daughter is right, and that they have no idea where Kelly might be. Alfred imagines himself driving around the city, aimless and confused, with a feigned angry expression, hating himself for not being very careful with his device.

"Anyways," she says, pulling out her phone from her dress pocket, scrolling through it, "I have taken the liberty to find him for you. Bypassing his security protocols and firewall, though not easy anyway, was very exciting to do. Also, I have actually been following him since he left, and right now, he is at a restaurant called Dancing Hen's House, located at 6th View, Loner Street, in Daxonhill. What an absurd name for a restaurant and a street." Tiana says, grimacing disgust for the names.

His eyes still on the road, "We will come to how you were able to find him later, but now, we have your brother to find."

"You are welcome, father."

Alfred grunts at her audacity and sarcasm, pressing harder at the acceleration pedal.

Few minutes later, they are at 6th View, Loner Street, making their way to the restaurant located on their right. At the same time, April and Kelly are coming out of the restaurant, smoothies in hand and sharing a laugh at what Kelly had said to her earlier. His gaze falls to the ground, unable to find its weight, when he sees his family approaching him.

April realizes he isn't looking happy anymore, and turns her gaze toward the direction he is looking at, and sees a man with dark hair and silvery shade at the base, a woman with blue eyes and elegant dressing, and a little girl, about her brother's age, expressionless with piercing, blue eyes like Kelly.

April imagines these people to be Kelly's family, but thinks why would he look shocked and bruised seeing them.

"Running has always not been the answer when dealing with things, at least, not in my book. And you, Kelly, I thought you would know better." Alfred tells them, walking with measured steps toward Kelly.

"Father, what are you doing here? What are you all doing here? Tiana?" Kelly asks, a discomforting rush of jittery anxiety hits him, making his body to spasm, though silently.

"Kelly, I tried to stop him, but he wouldn't listen. Please, do not escalate beyond what it already is," Geneva begs him.

Alfred looks at April with a pry and condescending eye, making her comfortable where she stands. She shifts and turns, hoping Kelly will explain what's happening soon. But, he isn't saying anything.

"So, this is the girl you left Anthera for? I thought she was actually worth it, how disappointing."

April furrows her brows, and tilts her head in confusion, her body feeling distant and disoriented from the words of the aged man before her. She says nothing, her thought being to walk away from there.

As though Kelly could read her mind, he takes her by

the hand, and begins walking away from them. He says nothing to his father, as he thought it best not to answer. It would only make matters worse.

"I wonder what number she may be? Is she the 8th, or 9th girl?" Alfred says, watching as Kelly slowly stop.

Tiana grimaces a face of confusion, looking at her mother, "What's father talking, mother?"

"Alfred? It's enough. Let's go. Let Kelly be."

"Or, is she the 10th perhaps? Had to know how many girls you have had under your sheets," he tells Kelly, meeting his gaze as he turns to him. Alfred doesn't seem moved by his stance or violent expression, "It's very hard to keep count. And, I am tired of watching you move from one girl or the other, all in the name of you loving her. I wanted to make this easy for you, telling you to stay home, but you have tied my hands and thrown to me to the floor, leaving me no choice. However this turns out, it's on you."

Kelly's chests starts to push and pull, and rising and falling, his eyes stormy with fear and a stale taste building up in his mouth. The things around him suddenly stop moving, he can't hear, he can't see them, even the very wind that pushes against his body can no longer be felt, and he feels everything has been cast to the fire.

He turns a set of pleading, blue eyes at April, she is not looking at him, she's not moving. She stands there staring distantly at his family, as though in a trance that has impeded her from moving. Kelly could feel her fear, the anger congealing inside of her, the emptiness that will follow, and blames himself. He blames himself for what she is going through, and will go through. And, at that point, right where they stand, he wishes time could have been kinder to him.

April turns her gaze at him, at Kelly, and he meets it, teary and full of regret. He tries to say something to her, but his words fail him, he tries to reach for her hand, but April pulls herself away, her tongue unable to say anything audible. Her chest is burning, her head is hurting, any minute with him and his family might drive her insane, she thinks to herself.

"April? April, wait!" Says Kelly, calling to her as she walks away.

CHAPTER TWELVE

From the time she left Kelly at The Dancing Hen's, her mind hasn't been in its best form and shape. Thoughts of worry, regret, angst, pity, abasement, and anything that related to.the incident and her actions, ruled April's mind throughout the rest of the day. She has cried more times than she could count, she has tried sleeping to wave the thoughts off, speaking to herself to calm herself down, screaming into a pillow to release the tension. And yet, her heart bleeds anytime she thinks about it, causing her to shed another skin of fresh tears.

She is with her family at the dining table, they are having dinner, and the once colorful air that surrounded them whenever they ate, was no longer there. It was like a part of them have been taken away, beyond arm length. And however they try to get it back, it always seems to evade them.

April's moody atmosphere has put a spectre of silence over the room, with only chewed food and spoons hitting against plates to be heard. Her family tries to guess what could be wrong, since April has refused to mention it to them. She has refused to talk to them even.

"Err, April?" her mother calls out to her with a gentle tone, "Your aunt called today, aunt Maribelle, said she's got a promotion at her job, with nice pay too. Though, she was empathizing on that pay more than the promotion itself. Can you imagine that, hmm, April?" she adds, chuckling as she looks to others to join in.

An effort toward brightening April's mood, as Dareen knows April doesn't like her aunt much, so she will likely say something about the aunt and her promotion. Something about her being a hypocrite, a self-absorbed human with a sickening presumptuous attitude that's disgusting to even sit close to.

She felt April might say those things, but she didn't. She didn't as much raise her head from her food, she didn't tighten her lips as she used to, she didn't sneer and curse under her breath. April did none of that, and that bothered them all greatly.

Moments into their meal, a knock on the door comes pouring in, their attention shifts to it, except for April's. Gazes are exchanges, and they all feel it's for April. Dareen turns to April with a tender look, worried and drooping with concern, April still has her eyes on her food, fiddling it with her spoon.

"Are you expecting any visitors, honey?" she asks April.

"No." April replies with a melancholic tone.

"Maybe, someone might be here for you, remember last time?" Dareen asks her, putting up a smile.

"I do not want to see anyone." she replies, still in the same state.

Dareen bites her lips, dropping her spoon to the plate.

She thinks for a moment, her mind foggy as she tries to decide what else to do. She turns to Morris, but he isn't much of a help, he is eating his food and scrolling through his phone as his daughter's change of attitude is of no concern to him.

She gasps at the thought, pushing it aside so it doesn't disturb her. The knock comes through for the third, and Dareen grunts softly, nearing the end of frustration. Damien peers at his mother, and sees the tension building up on her face, and after some thoughts, he gets up.

"I will go check who it is, mom," he tells the mother, walking toward the door.

Dareen nods her head in appreciation at him, she then turns to look at Morris, he is still not paying attention to what's happening at the table. And she wishes his phone would catch on fire, that way, he will pay attention.

A while later, Damien comes back and stands near April, darting his eyes from his mother to April, looking a bit nervous. He hesitates to speak.

Dareen searches his face, unsure of what's wrong with Damien, "Well, who is it?"

"There is a person outside, said he's looking for April and would like to meet her right now. That he won't take much of her time, he said it will be brief, that he promise." He replies, though looking April's way as though saying the words to her.

April doesn't say anything, she dabs at her eye, wiping off a tear that was about to roll down. She sniffs inward, and scoops a little of the mashed potato pudding in her plate, taking it up to her mouth.

"April? Damien said you have a visitor." Dareen tells her.

"I said I do not wish to see anyone. I don't want to, and I don't feel like it. Tell the person to go and leave me alone." She blurts out.

"The person said he has something you might need, something that may make you feel better. It is almost as though he knows you are a mess." Damien tells her additional information he had withheld.

April exhales deeply, "Is it Nigel?"

"Didn't mention his name." Damien replies.

April's exhales again, this time, more calmly and relaxed, bracing herself up to meet whoever is bent on seeing her. She cleans herself up, adjusting her hair and wiping her eyes, wanting to cover up her moment of grief as she has not the strength to explain to anyone how she's feeling.

She gets done, and moves away from the table. April gets to the door, and hesitates before opening it, reconsidering her choices about coming out. She finally decides to go out to meet the person, opening the door and stepping out.

April enters into the cold, humid air of their Daxonhill neighborhood, she lowers her brows as she tilts her head from left to right, unable to see anyone. She gets confused and wonders if the person is playing pranks with her, she starts to get angry as she decides to go inside, and walk up to her room.

She makes to go inside, but stops, her heart skips a beat, something it does when Kelly is around or when he calls out to her. And in the humid air of the neighborhood, she hears Kelly's voice again. She hears her name again, April, fluid and well stressed, something she likes to hear from him, and her eyes start to water all over again. She turns to meet his gaze, on her right, walking out of a dark corner, hence the reason she couldn't see him earlier. Moments later, he comes fully into the view, looking into April's glistening eyes as it shivers under the bright florescent light.

He moistens his dry lips, and makes to say something, "I know you are angry, upset, and must have probably made up your mind that people like me are definitely not to be trusted. And that's fine, we humans do that when we are angry and bitter, bruised when something…or someone has hurt us. We lose whatever piece that held us together.

But, hear me out, whatever you heard earlier today, I just wanted to say…that it was all true. All of it."

April wheezes, and turns to walk into her home.

"But, it all changed, April!" he yells out, his voice bringing her to a stop, "It changed when I met you, and believe me when I say this, that no day passed, I didn't convince myself that was indeed holding a delicate flower in my hands. You are different from the tens of other Daxonhill girls I have met, and when I saw that flare in you, that light that burned brighter than others, I knew…I knew that you were all I needed.

And you are still all I need now, and if you do not want to forgive me, just know that I understand and I accept whatever comes after. I'm sorry, April. I'm sorry for hurting you this way."

April looks around her to realign her thoughts properly, holding back the tears that welled at the corners of her eyes, and no matter how much she wipes them, they always gathered up again.

She passes a tongue between her lips, her eyes on Kelly as he approaches her, "Was I actually among the girls you were going to use and dump?"

Kelly pauses, looking into April's deep, brown eyes. He hesitates to answer, but shakes his head as manages a reply, "And sad as it was, I can't say you weren't, April. But, I rescinded the idea a long time ago, you have to believe me."

"So, I was just another girl-toy for you? For your pleasure, isn't it?"

"No, at least, not anymore. That was in past now, I wouldn't be here if—"

"And I liked you!" she bellows, the sides of her lips shaky and drooping, "I liked you, Kelly. I thought about you, I imagined you with me in another world where we will spend our lives together. I always hoped for the time we would meet again, even when I attempted walking back or walking away, the thing I had for you always made me stop. It made me weak, but it was because I liked you.

I thought you were different from them, how I want to believe it—"

"And I am sorry for that, April."

"No, Kelly, no. I was only a fool not to believe what my frienda told me, I feel so stupid not listening to them, seeing as cynical bigots who weren't ready to change their thinking and beliefs about you, about your people. And, for many years, they have been seeing me as myopic and shallow, and now, I feel undeserving of their presence. How stupid I have been."

"It is fine to hate me for what I have done, or intended to do, but from a place of sincerity and honesty, I tell you that all has passed, and even if we don't get back together again, know that not all of us are as bad as we are painted to be. We are human, prone to errors like machine, some say humans are the most peculiar machines to ever have evolved, we are fallible, we can do mistakes, and most times, those mistakes can be so stupid and capricious, it might lead to a perilous end. Severing apart a bond, or a budding bond, just like ours now.

But, what makes us different from the AIs we build, the machines with mechanical arms and legs, is the ability to realize our mistakes and make amends, just like what I am doing now. Please, April, I beg you to see the light in what I am saying and know my heart is in your hands. I gave it to you the day I walked to your school, seeing you not walk away from me convinced me you were different. And most girls that I follow, just wanted to know how being under sheets with a nerd will feel like, and I gave it to them. I will admit I liked it, which made me continue, but when I met you, I had the same thought, but it changed on our second meeting. It all changed."

April's eyes are deep inside Kelly's, holding on them as he spoke, she could see the tint of sincerity in them, the shame and guilt that filled his eyes. And she wanted to believe, she really wanted to, but her thoughts kept fighting inside of her, a battle she isn't able to bring to a stall. She feels conflicted, wounded, and the anger in her still boils like water in a geyser.

She feels tired about it all, not knowing what else to say to him, she turns toward the door and walks to it, ignoring Kelly's pleas and calls for her name.

"Go home, Kelly. Goodbye."

April walks into the house, trotting toward the stairs as her parents' words of concern fall stiffly against her ears, going unheard and unreplied. She goes up to her room, and she sinks into her bed, crying and screaming briefly into her pillow.

She takes her head out from the pillow some moments later, her hand folded and cradling her head as places it on them, she stares out distantly at the stars as they shiver in the night sky. She thought recalling the moments she and Kelly had shared, the laughs and the jokes, the romantic treatment she had received. She remembers the sense of epiphany to become her best self, to match his brains and wits and his personality, a conscious effort she had made toward being an amazing partner and lover to him. She liked him, she really did, but as she lies in her bed, staring at tiny dots of light burning billions of miles away, she can help but think how foolish she must have been.

April wipes her tears, and reaches for her phone, she swallows as she runs her tear-bloated eyes through the names of her contacts. She taps Nigel, placing a call across to him.

"Hey, Nigel," she says when the call gets picked, "Are you doing anything now? I was wondering if we could hang out together, this night?"

"Are you serious right now, April?" Nigels asks on the other end.

"Yes," she replies, trying to sound sane, "Can you come over to my place? You know, so we can—"

"Yes, April, I will be there soon. I am coming right now." Nigel says hurriedly, hanging up even before April could take the phone away from her ear.

April drops the phone to the bed, closes her eyes shut for a minute, recollecting her thoughts and bringing them to a place of serenity and peace. A while later, she gets out of bed, and starts to ready herself for Nigel's arrival.

After 10 minutes getting ready, dressed in a black, skinny jean, a red jacket with a top underneath, and a pair of black boots. She walks downstairs and sees her parents and brother in the living room, she keeps on walking without looking in their direction.

"Mom, dad, I will be back soon, just going out with a friend." She tells them.

"Alright, honey, don't stay late." Her mom tells her.

She goes outside, and finds Nigel already packed. And she walks up to his car, and gets in, she doesn't say anything to him, and so does he. He pushes at the ignition, and the car roars to life, and slowly, he drives into the road and out of the neighborhood.

Few feet away from April's house, way behind Nigel's car, Kelly saw April enter the car. He knows the person behind the wheel, and has seen them together due to his peculiar habits, but the extent of their relationship is what he doesn't know.

Yet, he feels bruised about it, seeing April get into his car. He feels she is trying to forget him, a reality he is still trying to come to terms with, to learn not to be with him, to throw him to the wind to wither. And he understands, though it hurts like thorns piercing into his heart. Kelly rises from the concrete sidewalk he is sitting on, and with his hands in his pockets, and sullen eyes on the ground, he walks home, never to come looking for April again.

CHAPTER THIRTEEN

It's gym practise in Daxonhill High, boys and girls have been divided up into teams and placed to face each other in a game of dodgeball. The gym instructor has instructed the students on what to do, and has told them how clean the game must be. The students have acquiesced to the rules, taken their positions, and with sly looks on their faces, they begin the game of dodgeball.

How it would have been grand for the instructor's words to be heard and heeded, for as the students throw their balls at each other, they throw with the intent to come out victorious. And most times, this feeling of wanting to win and come out on top can go south, and a student will end up getting hurt and sometimes, bruised. However, the instructor knows this, but it has become more like a tradition to tell them what to do, even when none of it will be followed.

As they play, April watches them from up the sloppy seats in the large room they are in, looking over the basketball court where the others play their game. Her mind is clearer now, though she used her state of being to get exemption from joining them at the dodgeball game. She feels lighter than she had felt two days ago, her breath more fluid and less noticed, she can think clearly now. And she has been doing a lot of thinking.

Moments later, Reilly joins her, hyper and jumpy and in a good mood. April turns to look at her, ahe furrows her brows as she wonders what could be making Reilly this happy.

"Okay, should we be celebrating something?" April asks her, looking at the students below, then at Reilly.

"Nothing, I just feel good, that's all. Shouldn't I feel good again?" Reilly retorts back.

April smiles, "So, what's up with lately? Done with your project yet?"

Reilly raises her mouth upwards, thinking for a moment, "The project is going great, I guess. I mean, my partner has been very helpful lately, doing most of the work and compiling it too. All I do is write sometimes, and give her what she needs when she needs it, and that's it. She has been lovely, I must say."

April nods softly, shifting her gaze to the legs, "And what's her name again, Daisy, right?"

"Yeah, her name's Daisy, but I call her Dee, hope it's not too weird?"

April shakes her head, "No, it's not weird at all, I don't find it weird at all."

"Oh, it's alright then. So, what about your project, how is it going? Any progress with Nigel?" Reilly with curiosity filling her voice.

April shrinks where she is, "Project is going fine, hasn't been much of a problem, I believe. But there's something else."

Reilly narrows her gaze at her, looking into her face, "Okay, what's it?"

April sighs, "Promise me you won't raise your voice too much."

"I promise, now say it."

"I and Kelly had a fight, and I think that may have ruined our…our friendship," she tells her slowly, fiddling with her hands.

"Did you just say friendship? Why would you want to be friends with him in the first place?"

"I told you not to shout."

"I am not shouting, this is not me shouting."

April groans as Reilly keeps raising her voice, though no one is looking their way, she feels the whole school can hear them. She plunges her face into her hands as she regrets telling Reilly what has been on her mind.

"Yes!" April blurts out, stern in her words, "I am friends with a nerd, just deal with it already. There's typically nothing wrong with it, nothing! There is nothing bad in having one as a friend, and there are definitely people out there, in this city, with friends who are nerds just like Kelly. I really don't see why you should be making it a big deal, Reilly. I know you hate them and don't trust me, which is okay, but please, not all should be tagged the same thing. It's annoying, and I…kinda hate it too."

April and Reilly stare sternly into each other's eyes, emotions pouring out through them like water from a fountain. April feels she hasn't done more damage to the friendship she has with Reilly, a friendship they have shared for years they both can't remember.

But, April also knows that friends can fight, and if that can happen, surely they can outgrow each other as well. Though she hopes it doesn't lead to that.

"If that's the way you want it, April, so be it. I want no part of it," Reilly days defiantly.

April searches her stern and rigid face curiously, she sees that Reilly has been bruised by her words, she lets her be as she shifts her gaze at those hurting each other with dodgeballs.

***

At a chess club in Anthera, Kelly is with his friends again, talking over a game of chess. The place is quiet, serene, and oozes nothing but class and quaint interior. Chairs clothed with brown leather, small round tables where the chess boards are placed, and black and white marble floor gracing the entire ground they stand and match on. In the background, classical music is been played to match the mood of the room, going hand in hand to aid the critical thinking that goes into securing a win in the game.

Kelly has his eyes keenly on the board, contemplating his next move to evade one of his chess pieces from being taken. After so much thought on it, he decides to move the knight two steps sideways, that way, he has more time to think through his move again.

"Afraid that you might lose?" he asks him smiling, trying to get under his skin, while moving a chess piece.

"I do not intend to lose, Edward, I have my strategies and with them, losing is not an option," Kelly tells him, without raising his gaze.

"That's good, Kelly, that shows that you are confident. And even if you lose, you won't waver, as you go on to re-calibrate your moves next time," Edward says, laughing at the end of his statement.

"I do not think I will be the one recalibrating my moves, but you. Only time will tell."

"Hmm, I have been thinking," says Edward, while he waits for Kelly to make his move, "That Daxonhill girl that you like, have you two been seeing? It's been over a week you came home, and you haven't gone back to her city."

"I have no business with her anymore, and I wish not to speak of her. Let's play our chess, please."

"Why does it sound like you have gone into a squabble with the girl? Like there is a fracas between you and her? I mean, listening to you speak suggests exactly that."

Kelly moves a chess piece one step forward, "There's fracas between us, we just don't talk anymore, and I do not wish to speak about her too. I am done with her, and that's it. It is not like I got anything from her."

Edward stops playing, looking into Kelly's face as he maintains his gaze on the chess. He searches his face and the manner Kelly uses to avoid the talk of the Daxonhill girl, knowing something is amiss, but Kelly doesn't deem it fit to say anything about it.

Kelly takes his gaze up, his brows arches inward in a curious grimace as Edward isn't playing anymore.

"Why have you stopped countering my moves?" Kelly asks.

"I stopped because I am trying to understand why my friend is hurt, and he doesn't want to talk about it."

Kelly lips lowers in a sneer, he grunts and groans as he reclines back into his chair. He seems tired that Edward is persistent to talk about an issue he is trying to forget, an issue he wishes to put behind him and cast it to the fire to burn to ashes. And one of the ways he has chosen not to rekindle the pain he has been pulling back, is to not talk about April, or mention anything about her to anybody. But, he feels that cannot be possible anymore as his friend now knows.

"Okay, you want the truth so badly? Fine, I will give you the truth. We had a little fight, a little misunderstanding, where I was at fault, and her fear about me, about us the nerds, escalated, and she stopped calling me or wanting to see me. And since she doesn't want to, I know well enough, not to disturb a lady who doesn't want your friendship anymore. There, there is the truth, happy now? Good, let's play."

"Woah, that was fast, and not only that, I figured that

what you two might be going through might just be a minor roadblock of some sort. Yes, she might have said or shown that she doesn't want to see you again, but she's a lady, they are often like that when they are in pain. In fact, everyone is, if you ask me."

Kelly narrows his eyes at his friend, staring at with a tight lips and thoughtful eyes, he taps his foot impatiently on the floor, hesitating a reply, he groans painfully as though about to say something he has been withholding, spilling it out nevertheless.

"So, what are you insinuating?" he asks finally.

"What I am saying is try and go back to her, talk to her and see if she still hates you. Chances are, she doesn't, she's only going through a phase that's a little too unnerving for her right now. For all I know, she might have healed already, you just have to go check up on her, like a doctor for a sick patient. Am I communicating here?"

Kelly twirls his mouth around his face, tapping his fingers on the armrest of the chair he is sitting on, thinking of Edward's words. He might have a point, April might have healed at the moment, waiting for him to come back. But the thought of seeing another person, another guy with her is what he is not ready to handle, he can't handle it, and would risk seeing it for any reason. Imagining such a scenario is enough to hurt him, going to her and meeting them together is enough to sink him into the ground.

He sits upright, shrugging the thoughts away and bending toward the table with the chess board, he tells his friend, "Let's stop this nonsense talk, I have a game to win tonight."

CHAPTER FOURTEEN

Kelly is in the dining area with his parents, they are having lunch, but not with the atmosphere that once ruled the mood of everyone. Now, the place is cold and dark, even when enough lights are pouring in from outside, the tension mostly coming from Kelly being away from home for more than a week, causing his parents to have something else to worry about.

'If he isn't at Daxonhill, where else will he be?' Alfred, Kelly's father, would ask, his exasperated voice echoing throughout the walls of the house.

Ever since Kelly came back two days ago, he knows things haven't been as smooth as it is, but he is no longer angry at him anymore, or angry at his sister for showing them where he was. He was at a better place of thought, and believes father's coming might have changed something in him. Regardless, he still wants his family to act like what it is. A family.

"So, I have got this craziest story, who wants to hear it?" Kelly asks them at the table, looking forward to their positive response.

His mother and sister turn their gaze at him, both still

eating their meals. Tiana lowers her gaze back to her without saying a word, feeling a bit guilty for what she had done.

"Kelly, we are eating, and you know what we have said about talking while eating, it is–"

"I know, mother. it is a good habit, I know, but you will surely enjoy it, trust me. It happened to me last week." Kelly tells her convincingly.

"I will like to hear the story," Tiana says, making Kelly smile. She turns to her mother to see her with a stern look on face, "He said it's the craziest story, how many crazy stories have you heard in your lifetime, mother? How many?" she asks her mother, in her own little way to convince.

Kelly gets a good ahead from his mother, he looks over at his father, and he sees he isn't paying attention to what's happening on the table. Though, Kelly feels he is listening.

"So, at my friend's place," he begins, his voice a near baritone, "In his condominium where I stayed for a while, he told me he wanted to play chess, I said alright, bring out the chess pieces, let's play, and that was when he said not here, Kelly. I was surprised that he said that, saying we won't play chess here, like where else would we go to play it?

Anyways, he mentioned a place, Chess and Zest club, and I was flabbergasted that a place such as this existed in Anthera, and I didn't know."

"There are a lot of places that are not too talked about, either they are for exclusive owners or high paying citizens of our city. Either way, you better be rich."

"Hmm, you don't say," Kelly says to her sarcastically, tilting his head queerly and with a sly grimace on his face.

"I am so sorry, brother, you can continue."

"Anyway, we got dressed, and left for Chess and Zest, arriving a few minutes later because his place was only 25 minutes from the club. And when I entered the club, I felt like the little man who has entered a place of class and affluence. Anyway, we got underway playing our game, having a little chit chat and some drinks at the side. Two young fellow walked into the club, sneering lips and eyes like it could produce diamonds if it could. They seemed arrogant in a way."

"Hoo, I smell trouble here." Says Tiana, wanting more of the story.

Kelly continues, "So, these two gentlemen, with the clothes of fine tailoring and smell of the best perfumes, approach us and after looking at us like rodents that need to done away with, asks us (and I thought it very funny), 'Would you please mind going over to the otherside of the floor, at those seats over there.

I and Edward glanced at each other, wondering where they might have come from. We have had people do the most annoying thing, but this one was a real blow to the chin. We looked at each other for a moment, we didn't say anything to them, we didn't make a sound as we wouldn't want them believing we gave them importance. And continued our game.

After a while and series of murmuring from the two men, they turned to us again, and one of them said to us, 'feel free to select some table here and make us of them, if it is the fear of paying another buck for it, don't worry, I will get that settle for you. Am I clear about this?' Edward looked at me and smiled and smiled back, knowing that these men had no idea who they were messing with."

"Who? You or Edward?" Geneva asks with keen interests.

Kelly's attention shifts to her, he glances quickly at his father and finds him somewhat paying attention and he smiles inwardly.

He thinks for a moment, "Both of us, but mostly my friend. He is way richer than I can be. Maybe when I start working for a tech company as well, or build mine, then I will be on his level."

"Even greater." His father chips in affirmatively.

Kelly searches his father's face, smiling a tender smile, "Yes, father."

Now, he is convinced they are back, back to the way they were, and everything has faded into the air that dust on a windy day. Kelly sits there thinking of the other possible things he should be able to do as his father now speaks with him and highly of him too, but soon gets snapped back when Tiana tells him to continue and finish up the story.

"Yeah, sure-sure," he says, adjusting on his chair, "Alright, so after they had said such words to us, my friend stopped playing the game, and he sat back into the soft leather chair he was in, and he looked up at the one that said those words, he asks him, 'and I reckon you may be thinking I got this table for how much? 40,000 grand? 60,000? 70,000 grand perhaps?'

The man smiled at Edward, a very demeaning smirk if you ask me, one I wouldn't be too pleased to look at for long, but Edward was patient, I love him for that. The man replied, 'This is my favorite spot, boy, so it's either you quote your price and leave, or our money will get security and they will chase you out.' The other one beside added, 'Hence the reason we are doing this as civilized and as sane as we can, can't we all agree?'

Edward laughed, but I was getting annoyed where I sat. I turned to the two fellows beside me, and I stared them dead in the eye, 'We are not going to leave this table for you just because it's your favorite, and we are definitely not going to leave it just because you have money to throw around. Do you...' I want to say something Edward held me, telling me to calm down, and I stopped, looking out for answers, but he didn't provide any. Then, he did what made me a little angry."

"What?" asked Tiana hastily, wanting to know what next comes after, "Teeth came flying as a fight broke out between the four of you, and you and Edward came out victorious at the end. There was a lot of blood, but it was worth it, wasn't it?"

Kelly arches his lips up, putting on a smug, satisfied look, he replies his sister, "Even better."

"What could be better than fighting two arrogant human beings to the point of submission and epiphany on their part? What exactly?" she chirps with confusion on her face.

"I said even better, because at the end, Edward made them pay twice the amount he paid for the table, an amount he also inflated, and we walked out of there with more money than we could ever use in a month. Now, tell me, what's sweeter than that."

Tiana groans, "You have a point. So, how much did they pay?"

"Edward told them he paid 160,000 grand for the table, and it turns out they have a lot of money flying around, so they paid twice the amount of that, and Edward gave 200,000 grand out of it. I feel so rich right." He smiles to himself, his body feeling lighter and lighter.

"Your friend was very smart at handling them, he used them to get what he wanted, and in the end, he succeeded. A very smart choice."

"Certainly, mother." Kelly responds to his mother, with his mouth full of food.

"Kelly Alfred, what have we said about speaking while eating? Do you want to choke yourself? Now, drink a lot of water to wash down whatever excess food might not have gone down. We need your oesophagus clear and clean. Don't put me through a panic attack."

Kelly gulps down a glass of water, dropping it on the table as he is done, "I won't, mother. You will be fine till you see me turn 40."

The mother smiles, going back to her meal. Kelly catches the expression on all the faces at the dining table, content that he has been able to make them all relax, realizing that his family matters more to than any other person out there. And that, without the warmth of his mother, the advice of his father, no matter how harsh, and the problematic persistence and cunning gimmicks of his sister, no one gives him as much satisfaction as they do. A realization his friend's advice has been able to make him see.

He lets out a breath of satisfaction, taking his food in his hand, he moves away from the table, "Alright, everybody, I will be going to my room now. If you need me, I will be upstairs."

He tells them, walking to his room. They only nod at his statement, no one said anything, and he doesn't need their reply, knowing that they were back was enough to keep him in a good mood.

Over at Daxonhill High, April is still trying with frantic efforts to look for the missing part of their project, she hasn't been able to find it ever since, and it is driving to the point of insanity.

"Why do you even want this in the project anyway? It is not that relevant, at least that's the way I see it," Nigels tells her, his hand behind his head, leaned back in his chair in the library, staring at the ceiling.

"But, it is to me. I know it is somewhere online, just hidden from my very eyes. If only we have knowledge of how computers work and how to find things on the internet, we should be able to find it."

"And what if it is not on the internet? Or, in any book at all, online and offline? And no one has written about these animals' time of existence, what would you do? Form yours?" he asks her, giving her a side glance.

"I might just actually do that, being the first to do that shouldn't hurt, should it?"

"That's the nerds' job to do that, we shouldn't bother ourselves with things like this."

Still have her eyes peering closely at her computer screen, "Turns out I won't be the first person to record the dates of these creatures, but also the first Daxonhill folk to do it. History made."

Nigel shakes his head, feeling a sense of pity for April, "You amuse me sometimes."

She moves over to a book, brown and old and dusty, "I know, I amuse myself at times too, Nigel."

April's attention soon switches to her phone, a notification bell has just rung from her phone, and she picks it up to see what it could be, or who it could be. She takes it up to her face level, peering at her screen, she sees it's a message from an anonymous person, sent to her through one of her social media accounts.

She opens the message and hopes it isn't one of those unsolicited messages guys send girls, thinking it's an appropriate thing to do. But, she doesn't see that, and it gladdens her greatly to see this. She sees a link to a website, and new set of fears creep into her like cold air through a crack in the door.

Skeptical, she opens it up anyway, and as she reads although the webpage, her heart and mind keeps spreading and spreading, a smile forming on her face that she could no longer hold in her joy. She jumps into the air, screaming and gushing over her phone, this startles Nigel as he almost falls back on his chair. He steadies himself as thick as he could, bug-eyed and holding the table for balance, he glares at April asking her what happened, but she doesn't answer him.

After some moments of jittery emotions and happy sensation, with the right amount of morphine been released in her body, April with a wide smile, sets herself to sit back on the chair, ignoring dazed and confused eyes that stared at her from a distance.

She tries to calm herself to a crawl, "Okay, okay, errm, yes, I just saw, right now, a link that showed everything I have been looking for, that we have been looking for, crossing out days of constant search and sleepless nights of trying to find it."

Nigel takes the phone from her, scrolling through the site, he smiles, "But, who sent this? Did you tell anyone about the project, someone who might feel like helping?"

April shakes her head, still grinning, "Err, no, I didn't tell anyone, except Reilly. It was only Reilly I have discussed my project with, she is the only soul who knows I haven't found a missing piece in my research."

"Do you think she might have sent this?" Nigel asks, putting the phone up to her face.

April scowls her brows in deep thought, trying to figure out if it was Reilly that sent the link. And when she couldn't come up with a better explanation for it, she dismissed it.

"Can't possibly be her, if she was the one she would have sent it through her account, and not an anonymous account. I literally don't know this person."

"Hmm, sounds very weird, if you ask me. However, do make sure to ask Reilly if she was the one, or if she discussed it with someone who might have helped her send it to you. You never can tell."

April stares at Nigel for a moment, she nods her head, agreeing to his words, "Alright, on our way home today, I will ask her, she should have answers."

"Alright. Now, that's away, I was thinking," he says to April, bringing her attention back to him, "There is this new place in town, they said it's for only the people of Daxonhill, and no nerds will be allowed in. And even when they get in, they will be sniffed out quickly, and thrown out. So, I was thinking maybe you might want to go check out the place with me this evening, what do you say?" Nigel asks her.

April's breath suddenly stops at her chest, her throat constricting in its walls, making it a daunting task to breathe properly again. She doesn't know what to make of Nigel's request, but she knows going to a place where only her people will be in, doesn't seem like a fit and nice place for her to be. She can only imagine what they would be doing, saying, and eating, and for someone like her who is going through a paradigm shift, she sees it as a farfetched activity to indulge in.

"Ahh, Nigel, I am sorry, I can't. I really cannot go with you, I have this thing I am doing with my family and–"
"Oh, it's fine. Maybe some other time then."

"Yeah, some other time. But, I can let Reilly know if she would like to go, she kinda likes those kinds of places."

Nigel nods, considering April's words, "Yeah-yeah, I think you can tell her. If she's okay with it, then I will come pick her up."

"Beautiful, she will be very delighted to hear this, Nigel, take it from me."

Nigel says nothing, he only smiles at April as she goes back to her phone, writing down what she has gotten into the notepad before her with a broad smile on her face.

After school hours, April and Reilly go their separate ways in their neighborhood, with Reilly telling April she wasn't the one who sent the link. She was confused about it, but later shrugged it off, she didn't see the need to bother herself with things like this. As she bade farewell to Reilly, about to walk into their front lawn and up to the porch, she feels her phone ring, and pulls it out, peering at the screen.

Someone is calling her, a name she hasn't seen in a while. It is Kelly calling, a faint, tender smile escaping from her lips, as her eyes squint under the bright, yellow sun.

She takes the call, "Hey."

"Turn to your left," he tells her.

She does so, and a broad smile breaks out on her face. April sees Kelly walking up to her, his hands in his pocket, wearing a well tailored trouser, a woolen vest and a button-up T-shirt underneath. He has his light brown hair in a different style, low and oiled properly. April walks up to him as well, her legs wanting to run to him but she restrains herself from doing so, it is unladylike, she tells herself. Though, if she wanted, she would do it, but for the name of self-worth, she will put it aside today.

Now standing before one another, eyes locked, heart racing and hammering against their chest, hands wanting to reach up to their faces, they take a moment to soak in all the energy they are exuding from within themselves, letting themselves know, as though by tacit knowledge, that they still care for one another.

"I am sorry, April. For everything."

"I think you have already apologized way too many times already. Sending that link kinda puts it as a cherry on-top."

Kelly lets out a laugh, looking down at his shoes, then looking up to her, "Do you mind if we go hang somewhere? That's if–"

"I don't mind." April interjects quickly, her eyes still and anxious, and on Kelly's face.

Kelly stretches out his hand to her, his anxiety over his action beating against his body like iron over a surface. April stares down at the hand, hesitating to take it, but with every heartbeat her heart gives off, it beats closer to Kelly. She looks up to his gaze, his blue eyes enthralling her as she swims in them, she extends her hand as well, lacing it together with his, and at that moment, two worlds became one.

F
— ✕ —
M